Melanie Milburne read her first Harlequin novel at the age of seventeen, in between studying for her final exams. After completing a master's degree in education, she decided to write a novel, and thus her career as a romance author was born. Melanie is an ambassador for the Australian Childhood Foundation and a keen dog lover and trainer. She enjoys long walks in the Tasmanian bush. In 2015 Melanie won the HOLT Medallion, a prestigious award honoring outstanding literary talent.

Books by Melanie Milburne

Harlequin Presents

The Return of Her Billionaire Husband

Once Upon a Temptation
His Innocent's Passionate Awakening

Secret Heirs of Billionaires
Cinderella's Scandalous Secret

Wanted: A Billionaire
One Night on the Virgin's Terms
Breaking the Playboy's Rules
One Hot New York Night

Visit the Author Profile page
at Harlequin.com for more titles.

To all the wonderful people out there who adopt or foster children and give them a happy and loving home. And a special message of love and heartfelt empathy to those who can't have their own biological child.

Emmie waved her hand toward the velvet-covered chair opposite her desk. "Please, take a seat."

"Thank you." Matteo's deep voice sent another shock wave of awareness through her, and so, too, did the sharp citrus top notes of his aftershave.

Emmie sat back down before her trembling legs gave way beneath her. She had no idea why this man was having such a potent effect on her. She'd met dozens, hundreds, of men in her line of business and not one of them had caused her body to react like a starstruck teenager in front of a rock star. Even seated, Matteo Vitale was so tall that her neck muscles pinched as she craned her neck back to maintain eye contact.

"So, how may I help you, Mr. Vitale?" She activated her best businesslike tone, but something about the glint in his dark blue eyes was cynical, perhaps even a little mocking.

"You're a professional matchmaker, correct?"

"Yes. I individually profile my clientele and help them to find a partner who will be perfect for them in every—"

"I need a wife."

Dear Reader,

While the first COVID-19 lockdown was on, I immersed myself in my favourite books and the movies and television productions inspired by those books. One of them was Jane Austen's *Emma*. I watched the newest movie three times!

It made me want to write a story about a professional matchmaker, so Emmie and Matteo came to life. Matteo had already appeared, off the page, in the second book of my Wanted: A Billionaire miniseries—*Breaking the Playboy's Rules*. He intrigued me, even though, at that stage, I had only given him a name and a career. Some subsidiary characters are like that––they insist on their own story.

The irony of a matchmaker falling in love with the very person they are trying to match appealed to me in a comedic sense, but the backstories I gave Matteo and Emmie are truly heart-wrenching. That's why they deserve their happy-ever-after so much. Grief and loss and cancer and infertility are tough issues to address in a romance novel, but that is the beauty of this genre—we deal with life's most perplexing issues and our beloved characters triumph in the end.

Best wishes,

Melanie Milburne xxx

Melanie Milburne

THE BILLION-DOLLAR BRIDE HUNT

HARLEQUIN
PRESENTS

HARLEQUIN®
PRESENTS®

Recycling programs
for this product may
not exist in your area.

ISBN-13: 978-1-335-56878-6

The Billion-Dollar Bride Hunt

Copyright © 2021 by Melanie Milburne

This edition published by arrangement with Harlequin Books S.A.

For questions and comments about the quality of this book,
please contact us at CustomerService@Harlequin.com.

Harlequin Enterprises ULC
22 Adelaide St. West, 40th Floor
Toronto, Ontario M5H 4E3, Canada
www.Harlequin.com

Printed in U.S.A.

CHAPTER ONE

EMMALINE WOODCROFT WAS basking in the glow of yet another successful match between two of her dating agency clients when her secretary-cum-receptionist, Paisley, came into her office and informed her she had a walk-in who insisted on seeing her immediately.

'Male or female?' Emmie asked, putting her mobile phone back down on the desk.

Paisley pressed her back firmly against Emmie's office door, as if worried the client would stride in without waiting for permission. 'Male.' There was a slightly breathless quality to her voice and she added, 'Tall, very tall, good-looking. Italian, I think, going by the accent. Designer suit. But why he would want to engage a professional match-making service is beyond me. I'd have him in a heartbeat if I wasn't already engaged.'

A tingle of intrigue tiptoed across Emmie's

scalp on tiny stilettoed feet. A new client was always a good thing and a handsome one a bonus. And, given he was a walk-in, it confirmed to her that setting up a small bricks-and-mortar London office as well as her online platform had been a good idea. Spontaneous decisions to engage her match-making services often produced the best results. It was when people let their guard down, inspired by an in-the-moment impulse. 'Send him in.'

Paisley's eyes sparkled and she said *sotto voce*, 'Brace yourself, Emmie. You're not going to believe how off-the-scale handsome he is. He quite took my breath away.' She disappeared out through the door. A few moments later the door opened again, and a tall suited man stepped into Emmie's office and closed the door behind him with a firm click that sent a shiver coursing down her spine.

'Ms Emmaline Woodcroft? Matteo Vitale.'

If his looks hadn't been enough to send her senses spinning, the mellifluous tone of his voice with its distinctive Italian accent more than finished the job. At least six-foot-four but possibly half an inch or so more, he made her office seem tiny. Well, tinier than it already was. He had olive-toned skin and thick jet-black hair that was neither short nor long but somewhere in between. He was clean shaven but his late-in-the-day stubble was generously distributed along the lean landscape of his jawline and around his nose and mouth.

His mouth…

Emmie's breath stalled in her throat and a quiver went through her entire body. His mouth was the sort of mouth that would have sent Michelangelo rushing off to sharpen his chisels and restock on marble—a fuller lower lip with a thinner top one that was perfectly balanced by a deep ridge below his long, straight nose. It was a sensual mouth tempered by a hint of stubbornness, perhaps even a streak of ruthlessness. He had prominent ink-black eyebrows that would have met in the middle except for the two-pleated shallow groove of what looked to be a perpetual frown.

But it was his eyes that stopped Emmie's heart. With his Italian, olive-toned colouring she had expected dark-brown or hazel eyes, but they were an unusual shade of blue. They reminded her of an uncharted ocean, the unknowable depths giving no clue whether danger or buried treasure were hidden beneath.

Matteo strode across the carpet to stand in front of her desk, proffering his hand across the top. She slowly rose from her chair, because for some strange reason her legs were decidedly unsteady, and slipped her hand into the firm, warm cage of his. His long, tanned fingers pressed against hers and she gulped back an involuntary swallow. A tingle scuttled down the backs of her legs like a small startled creature.

'How do you do? Oh, and please call me Emmie.'

'Emmie.' Matteo said her name unlike anyone had ever said it before, his accent leaning a little heavily on the second syllable, making it sound more like *Em-meee*.

She had to remind herself to take back her hand because she was tempted to let it stay exactly where it was—captured in the warm, dry enclosure of his. She eased out of his light grasp, but her fingers tingled and the palm of her hand fizzed as if some strange energy had passed from his body to hers.

The energy moved further through her body like the powerful rays of a heat lamp, searing warmth that lit tiny spot fires in each of her erogenous zones. Zones that had lain dormant for so long it was a shock to feel them stirring into life now. Every millimetre of her skin was intensely aware of him. Aware of his towering presence, his penetrating gaze, his arrant maleness, his commanding, take-charge air.

Emmie waved her hand towards the velvet-covered chair opposite her desk. 'Please, take a seat.'

'Thank you.' His deep voice sent another shockwave of awareness through her, so too did the sharp citrus top-notes of his aftershave. Lemon and lime with a hint of something a little more exotic in the base notes that made her nostrils flare and her pulse throb.

Emmie sat back down before her trembling legs gave way beneath her. She had no idea why this man was having such a potent effect on her. She met dozens, hundreds, of men in her line of business and not one of them had caused her body to react like a star-struck teenager in front of a rock star. Even seated Matteo Vitale was so tall, her neck muscles pinched as she craned her neck back to maintain eye contact.

'So, how may I help you, Mr Vitale?' She activated her best business-like tone but something about the glint in his dark blue eyes was cynical, perhaps even a little mocking.

'You're a professional match-maker, correct?'

'Yes. I individually profile my clientele and

help them to find a partner who will be perfect for them in every—'

'I need a wife.' His blunt statement and the determined set to his mouth made her sit up straighter in her chair.

'I see. Well, then, you've come to the right person because I have successfully matched many couples who to date are still all happily together. Emmie's Magical Match-Ups has a track record I'm enormously proud of, and I know it's because I take the time to get to know each of my clients personally before I find them the love of their life.'

One side of his mouth lifted but it would be a stretch to call it anything near a smile. If anything, it matched the cynical glint in his eyes that seemed as perpetual as his frown. 'I don't want a long-term wife. Only one who will stick around long enough to provide me with an heir.'

Emmie blinked, wondering if she'd heard him correctly. She moistened her suddenly paper-dry lips and shifted slightly in her chair. 'So...you're not looking for love?'

'No.' His flat tone and cynical expression seemed to suggest he didn't believe the concept even existed. 'My father died recently and, unbeknownst to me, added a codicil to his will.

I will not be able to inherit my father's large estate in Umbria, which has been in my family for generations, unless I marry and produce an heir within a year.'

'I'm sorry for your loss—'

'Save your condolences. We weren't close.' His dismissive tone irked her and intrigued her in equal measure. What sort of relationship had he had with his father for his father to have added such an unusual codicil to his will? A large Umbrian estate meant there was a lot of money at stake, but Matteo Vitale didn't look like the sort of man who had to rely on a family inheritance to get by. His suit was bespoke, his shoes hand-stitched Italian leather, his beguiling cologne certainly not one of those cheap knockoffs you could pick up at any discount outlet.

His name rang a faint bell in her head... Hadn't she seen an article about him in the press a few months back about his work as a forensic accountant? He had uncovered a massive fraudulent operation during a high-profile divorce case. It had involved millions of pounds of cleverly hidden money but Matteo had uncovered it all. How galling it must have been to find out his father had hidden this codicil from him until it was too late to do anything to change his father's mind.

Emmie still had both her parents and, while she wasn't as close to her father as her mother since their divorce during her teens after her cancer diagnosis, she couldn't imagine not grieving for him. Nor could she imagine her father adding such a codicil to his will, because he of all people knew the last thing she could ever do was provide an heir.

'Look, Mr Vitale, I don't think I'm the right person to help you after all. My focus is on finding true love for my clients, not finding a womb for hire.' She began to push back her chair to bring the meeting to a close but something about his expression made her sit back down again.

The silence was palpable. It seemed to press in from all four corners of the room, robbing the air of oxygen until Emmie found it hard to expand her lungs enough to take a breath.

'I'm prepared to pay well above your normal fee.' His tone was coolly business-like. She knew she should inform him that no price would allow her to compromise her professional reputation by taking on a brief so far outside what she normally did for her clients.

But something about that ever-so-brief flicker of pain in his gaze captivated her.

Emmie studied him for a moment, scanning his features for any further sign of vulnerability, but there was none. He could have been carved from stone. 'How do you know I won't name a price more than your family estate is worth?'

'I've researched you. You're expensive but your clients get what they pay for. And, as you say, your success rate is commendable. I'll pay you three or four times what you normally charge.'

Emmie had done well with her business, better than she had expected, but it was an expensive service to run with increasing overheads. Plus, she had a mortgage, and she was helping her mother pay for her younger sister Natalie's therapy for an eating disorder that had started during Emmie's battle with cancer. It would be crazy not to at least consider Matteo's offer. His request might be a little outside her normal range of service but it was surely worth a try? Never let it be said she shied away from a challenge. Her history of chemotherapy was proof of that. 'You're a forensic accountant, right?'

His eyebrows lifted in mild surprise. 'Was that a wild guess?'

'I saw something about you in the press a while back,' Emmie said. Although the photo hadn't done him justice. Matteo Vitale had a commanding presence that no camera lens could ever capture. It wasn't just his imposing height or brusque manner—something about his eyes hinted at deeply buried pain. Pain that was so cleverly, determinedly hidden it took a special skill to recognise it.

And Emmie had that skill in spades. Her pain radar had been finely tuned by life's disappointments. There was a lot of truth in that old maxim 'it takes one to know one.' She saw in others what she hid so cleverly in herself. It caused other people pain to know about hers, so she had excised it. Denied it. Buried it. She could walk past a pram, smile at the mother and no one would ever guess the searing agony inside her heart that she would never hold her own child in her arms.

Her ovaries had been damaged during her chemo and no amount of wishing and hoping and bargaining and praying for a miracle was ever going to restore them. IVF and donor eggs had been mentioned by her doctors, but Emmie knew it wouldn't be the same as holding her own baby, seeing her own features and that of other members of her family in the child's features and personality. Emmie had decided that, if fate had decreed she was infertile, then she would accept it, as painful and heart-wrenching as it was. She had even convinced her parents and sister she had put that bitter disappointment behind her once and for all. It was too upsetting to see them worrying about her. Pitying her.

Emmie placed her hands on the desk in a clasped position. She felt compelled to find out everything she could about Matteo Vitale. He was like a complicated puzzle someone had presented her with, and she wouldn't rest until she solved it. 'I must admit, I'm finding it hard to understand why you even need my services, Mr Vitale. I mean, you're good-looking, and apparently rich enough to afford to pay me handsomely. I would have thought you'd have no trouble convincing any woman to do anything you asked her to do.'

'Do you include yourself in that statement?' His eyes held hers in a lock that sent a shower of unfamiliar sensations to her feminine core.

Emmie raised her chin a fraction and forced herself to hold his challenging gaze. 'No, I do not. I'm quite immune to charming men.' Or so she'd thought until he had walked through the door.

He glanced at her left hand, presumably to see if she was wearing a wedding or engagement ring. His gaze came back to hers, the dark slashes of his eyebrows slightly elevated. 'So, the premier match-maker is herself unattached. Interesting.' His tone was smooth, his expression again just shy of mocking.

Emmie stretched her lips into a tight smile and unclasped her hands and placed them on her lap beneath the desk. 'Mr Vitale, allow me to assure you my currently single status is a choice, not an unfortunate circumstance. My career is my focus and I pride myself on being totally available to my clients in order to give them the best possible service.'

Matteo continued to hold her gaze to the point of discomfort. Emmie was determined not to look away first but, as each microsecond passed, her heartrate increased and her breathing quickened. 'Good, because I don't have a lot of time to waste,' he finally said. 'I need to get this sorted as quickly as possible.'

'I'm tempted to say you can't hurry love, but clearly that's not applicable in your case.' Emmie rose from her chair and went to her filing cabinet and took out one of her glossy brochures and handed it to him over the desk. 'There are various packages you can sign on for, which are detailed in this brochure. The top-level package is probably the best option, given your time-pressure issue.'

Matteo held the brochure in one hand and with the other took out a pair of black-rimmed reading glasses from the inside pocket of his suit jacket and put them on. If anything, they made him look even more heart-stoppingly attractive. He leafed through the brochure, at one point pushing his glasses further along the bridge of his nose with his index finger, his forehead creased in deeper lines of concentration.

He lowered his glasses further down his nose and glanced up at her from over the top of them, his gaze so compelling she couldn't have looked away if she'd tried. She was vaguely conscious of holding her breath, wondering if he was going to walk out of her office without a backward glance, yet desperately hoping he wouldn't. Finding him a wife according to his brief would be a challenge but she had faced bigger ones—surviving Hodgkin's lymphoma as a seventeen-year-old being the primary one.

'I'll take the top-level package.' He closed the brochure and placed it back on the desk, taking off his glasses and slipping them back inside his jacket pocket. She caught a glimpse of his broad chest as he opened his jacket, his light-blue business shirt stretched over toned muscles.

Emmie blinked rapidly and tried to refocus. She resumed her seat and smoothed her skirt over her knees. 'As you can see from the outline there, I usually spend a bit of one-on-one time with my clients to get to know them. That way I can judge what sort of person would best suit them. I have a detailed questionnaire I ask my clients to fill in but I've always found it much more informative to actually see them in action, so to speak. Like at work, at leisure, socialising with their friends and family, if possible. Would that be agreeable to you?'

A hard light came into his gaze and his jaw shifted like a heavy lock clicking firmly into place. 'No can do the family. I'm an only child and my father is dead.'

'And your mother?'

He made a dismissive sound, part-snort, part-sigh. 'Haven't seen her since I was seven years old. She decided marriage and motherhood weren't for her.' He gave a 'couldn't care less' half-smile and added, 'I have no idea where she lives or even if she's still alive.'

Emmie frowned. 'I'm sorry. That must have

been very upsetting and destabilising for you as a young child.'

He shrugged one broad shoulder in a negligent fashion. 'I soon got over it.'

Emmie wasn't so sure that was entirely true. There was an aura of guardedness about him that suggested he wasn't comfortable allowing people too close. The walk-out of a mother at such a young age and with no contact since would be highly traumatic for a child. It would have created bonding issues, uncertainty, emotional withdrawal or lockdown and numerous other coping mechanisms that often, if not always, played out in adulthood. She had found the walk-out of her father when she'd been seventeen traumatic, but at least she still saw him occasionally. How much worse for a seven-year-old boy who had never seen his mother again?

'Some children are more resilient than others,' she offered. And then, on an impulse she couldn't quite account for, she added, 'How soon would you like to start with my programme? I'm fairly busy just now but—'

'Tonight.'

Her heart slipped from its moorings. 'Tonight?'

'Have dinner with me. You can pick my brain at your leisure.'

Emmie had an unnerving feeling he would find out more about her than she would about him. After all, he had built his hugely successful career on uncovering well-hidden secrets. His piercing gaze held hers and her pulse sped up again. 'Lucky for you, I happen to be free tonight. Would you like to invite a couple of friends along so I can see how you relate to them?'

A steely glint appeared in his eyes. 'Let's do this alone.'

Alone. Somehow the way he said that word made a frisson skitter over her flesh. Emmie disguised a swallow. Dinner alone with a client was not out of the norm for her. What was out of the norm was her reaction to the prospect of dinner with this particular client. Excitement, intrigue, nervous anticipation—all were fluttering about in her stomach like frenzied moths. 'You do have friends, yes?'

He gave an indolent smile that completely transformed his features, making him seem less serious, less tense and less guarded—more approachable and even more devastatingly attractive. 'But of course.'

'Are you worried what they might think of

you engaging the services of someone like me?'

'Not particularly, but I would rather keep my private life out of the press as much as possible.'

'You don't trust your friends?'

He gave a stiff quirk of his lips, his gaze inscrutable. 'I don't trust anyone.'

'That must be an occupational hazard of yours, I guess.'

'Perhaps.'

Emmie tucked a strand of her hair behind her ear, trying to disguise how much he was affecting her. Never had she been so interested in finding out more about a man's character. He was complex and closed off and compelling. She was as giddy as a teenager anticipating her first date. She had to get a grip. She was a professional match-maker and he was engaging her services to help him find a wife. She had no business being interested in him herself other than in a professional sense.

Getting to know him was essential to the success of the mission of matching him with a suitable partner. But, right at that moment, Emmie couldn't think of a single one of the female clients currently on her books who would suit his unusual requirement. Her clients wanted love. Didn't most people? They wanted connection and commitment and continuity.

'Yes, well, you'd be surprised at how few friends some people have these days, which is why finding a partner can be so difficult. Meeting someone through friends used to be a sure, safe way to meet a potential partner.' Emmie painted another smile on her lips and added, 'I've designed my business model by becoming that mutual friend for my clients. It's much more appealing to most of my clients than using a dating app.' She paused for a beat and added, 'I suppose you've tried the dating app approach?

'Not for my current situation.'

Emmie could feel a blush stealing into her cheeks at the thought of him hooking up with casual lovers via an app. She had no problem with casual sex, although she hadn't had a sexual partner for so long she was starting to wonder if her body would still know what to do if she happened to find someone she was interested in enough to do the deed.

You're interested in Matteo Vitale.

The random thought sent another wave of heat through her cheeks and she lowered her gaze from the disturbing intensity of his. 'Yes, well, your…erm…unusual specifications might attract the wrong sort of person. People often talk themselves up on social media apps.'

'Indeed.'

Emmie opened her desk drawer, pulled out a selection of forms and laid them in front of him on the desk. 'If you could fill in your details—phone number, email address, social-media channels and home address—I'll enter them into my system. I can assure you of absolute privacy. No one but myself has access to the personal information of my clients. And I only give your contact details to a potential partner once I've discussed it with you first. The only thing I outsource is the personality questionnaire, to a team of experts who analyse my clients' responses. It's a well-researched personality model that helps me decide who would best complement you.'

She handed him a card with a web address printed on it. 'Here's the link to the questionnaire. It takes about forty-five minutes and I get the results back in a week or so.'

Matteo took the card from her and slipped it into his jacket pocket. He took out a gold pen before she could pass him one off her desk and began to fill out the forms with enviable speed and efficiency. Emmie examined the dark scrawl of his handwriting. The bold strokes spoke of a man who had a determined streak, but the light flourishes on some of the consonants hinted at a romantic element to his nature. The other thing she noticed was he was left-handed. Approximately ninety percent of the world's population was right-handed, which to her made him seem even more unique.

But when he passed the completed forms back across the desk he did so with his right hand. 'There you go.'

'Are you mixed-handed or ambidextrous?'

'Mixed. I write with my left but do a lot of other things with my right.'

Emmie could only imagine what some of those things might be and how skilled he might be at doing them. He had broad hands, tanned and long fingered with neat, square nails and a dusting of dark hair along the back and each of his fingers. She found herself imagining his hands on her...not just a 'pleased to meet you' handshake but on her face, on her breasts, on her hips, on the most intimate part of her body.

Her female flesh stirred, tensed and tingled, as if every sensitive nerve was preparing itself for his touch. She squeezed her legs together under the table, but if anything, it made it worse. She pushed back from the desk and stood, hoping her cheeks weren't as pink as they felt. 'I mustn't keep you any longer, Mr Vitale. I'll get my secretary, Paisley, to book a restaurant for eight this evening. I'll text you the details and meet you there.'

He rose from the chair and his imposing height made her snatch in another breath. For someone so tall, he moved with leonine grace. He had a rangy rather than gym-pumped build, an endurance athlete rather than a sprinter, which gave her another clue to his personality. Driven, disciplined, goal-oriented, he wouldn't be afraid of hard work—in fact, he'd most likely thrive on it.

'I'll book the restaurant. And I'll pick you up.' His voice had an edge of intractability about it, which was another clue to his take-charge, stay-in-control personality.

Emmie decided against tussling with him about it, for she quite fancied seeing what car he drove and what sort of restaurant he would choose. Those would also be important clues she could use to assess his character. So, too, would visiting his home at some point.

'Fine. Just as well I don't live too far away.' She leaned down to scribble her address on the back of one of her business cards and handed it to him. He took it from her with the slightest brush of his fingers against hers and a jolt of electricity coursed through her body. She pulled her hand back and gave him a stiff smile. 'Till tonight, then.'

He gave a mock bow. 'I'm looking forward to it. *Ciao.*'

Emmie was looking forward to it too, far more than she had any right to.

CHAPTER TWO

MATTEO PULLED UP in front of a smart white Georgian town house in South Kensington and whistled through his teeth. Who knew operating a dating agency could be so lucrative? Emmie Woodcroft must be raking it in, even if she was just renting this place, let alone if she owned it. But all power to her, as long as she achieved what he was paying her to achieve—finding him a wife in a hurry.

He opened and closed his clenched hands on the steering wheel and took a steadying breath. He was still recovering from the shock of finding out about his father's last-minute addition to his will. Of course, he could buy several Umbrian estates and have money to spare, but he wanted his family estate. Wanted it so badly he was prepared to do whatever it took to secure it. He had spent years and more money than he wanted to think about restoring the rundown estate, and it was now producing olives, and grapes for award-winning wine. The crumbling villa of his childhood had been completely renovated and he had paid for all of it, his father having struggled financially for as long as Matteo could remember.

But, more importantly, it was the land on which Matteo's wife and child were buried and he would not be able to forgive himself if he let them down again by allowing the property to be sold. Eight years had passed since his pregnant wife had driven off to attend a pre-natal appointment he should have accompanied her to. They had argued about it that morning. He had been under time pressure from a complicated case he'd been working on for the Supreme Court in London, and had chosen to fly to London rather than stay in Umbria one extra day.

Matteo closed his eyes in a tight blink and clenched his hands around the steering wheel again until his knuckles protested. He opened his eyes and let out a ragged breath. His father had no doubt orchestrated the codicil on his will to force Matteo to marry again, even though Matteo had always sworn he would never do so. He wouldn't have married Abriana in the first place, but when she'd become pregnant during their brief on-again-and-off-again fling, he had offered her and their unborn child the protection of his name. It had seemed the right thing to do at the time but he often wondered if Abriana's unhappiness during their short time together had stemmed from knowing he hadn't been in love with her.

And now he must marry again without love being part of the equation. Because how could it be? He had no desire to love someone the way his father had loved his mother. The way *he* had loved his mother. He had learned from an early age how destructive deep love could be. He wanted no part of it. He cared about people, cared enough to put himself out for them, but he would never fall in love with anyone. He wondered if it was one of the few traits he had inherited from his mother. She'd given the appearance of love but hadn't felt it. The only time Matteo had come close to feeling it was when he'd seen the first ultrasound photo of his child. A flicker of something had stirred in his chest…

Matteo removed his hands from the steering wheel and unclipped his seat belt but he stayed seated in the car, taking in deep breaths that snagged at his throat like claws. His gut was in knots, his chest tight, his mind swirling with images of the scene of the accident that had killed his wife and tiny unborn son. Could he even face having another child, knowing there was a possibility it too could be taken away from him? Marrying again without love being part of the equation was asking for trouble. What if his new marriage ended up causing the same pain and destruction as his first? How could he bear it a second time—inflicting hurt and despair on someone who deserved so much better?

He could not forgive his father for putting him in such a painful and impossible situation. It smacked of meddling and manipulation and a cruel type of emotional torture he hadn't thought his father capable of. Yet here he was, doing all he could to fulfil the wretched terms of his father's will.

There was a sudden tap on the passenger window and Matteo was jolted out of his torturous reverie. He turned his head to see Emmie standing there dressed in a light-blue dress with a lightweight navy trench coat over the top. Her straight blonde hair was loose around her shoulders, reminding him of a skein of silk. Her periwinkle-blue eyes were highlighted by smoky make-up, including eyeliner, and her full-lipped mouth was a soft, rosy pink.

He'd had trouble keeping his eyes away from her mouth earlier that day. It was a mouth built for sensuality, its contours lush and soft and beautifully shaped. Her nose was straight with a slight elevation at the end, like a gentle ski-slope. Her cheekbones were another striking feature of her face—regal, aristocratic—and her skin was as clear and pure as cream.

He opened his door and went round to help her into his car. 'You should have waited until I knocked on your door.'

'I saw you pull up and thought I'd save you the trouble.'

What else had she seen? Matteo was starting to suspect Ms Emmie Woodcroft saw too damn much. He comforted himself that his car windows were tinted. She might not have seen much at all. He normally kept his self-recrimination sessions for when and where he could not be observed.

Emmie moved past him to get into the passenger seat and he caught a whiff of her perfume—a fragrant blend of bergamot and geranium with a base note of patchouli that danced past his nostrils, causing them to flare. He was so close to her he could have touched her, and was surprised at how much he wanted to. Ever since they had shaken hands in her office earlier that day, he had been able to feel the soft, gentle imprint of her hand against his. It had sent a shockwave through his blood, kicking up his pulse in a way he had not expected.

Matteo closed the passenger door for her, strode round to his side of the car and got back behind the driver's seat. 'Nice house. Do you rent it or…?'

'The bank owns most of it but I'm making good progress. Well, better than I expected when I first started in the business.'

He glanced at her as he put the car in gear. 'How long have you been in the business of match-making?'

She flashed a smile, showing brilliant white teeth that made something in his chest slip. 'Informally since I was a teenager, actually. I recognised I had a natural flair for understanding which people suited each other and decided to make a career out of it. I've been in business five years now.'

Matteo checked his rear vision and side mirrors and then pulled out into the street before he asked, 'What sort of qualifications have you got?'

'I've done a couple of online counselling

courses. I would have liked to do a psychology degree and a master's after I left school but things didn't work out that way.' Something about her tone made him glance at her again.

'Why?'

Emmie gave a shrug of her slim shoulders, her gaze trained on the road in front, but one of her hands was fiddling with the clasp of her evening purse in a restive manner. 'My schooling was interrupted during my teens.' She paused for a beat and continued, 'I spent a bit of time in and out of hospital.'

Matteo wondered what would have put her in hospital for an extended period but didn't want to pry. Some conditions were deeply personal. 'I'm sorry to hear that. Anything serious?'

There was another beat of silence.

'Nothing too serious.' She gave another smile that seemed a little forced and added, 'But it gave me a lot of time to learn stuff about people. To listen and observe. I even helped two young doctors to get together. They're still married with a couple of kids now. They send me a Christmas card each year.'

'So, you're a romantic at heart.'

'For other people, not for myself.'

'Which begs the question, why?'

Emmie opened and then closed the latch on her bag, the *click* as it shut overly loud in the silence. 'I'm helping you find a wife. You don't need to worry about my single status. I'm perfectly happy with my life as it is.'

Matteo knew better than to think that all women wanted the marriage and babies package. Many lived happy and fulfilling lives with neither partner nor children but something about Emmie's body language was out of tune with her words. It was like hearing the wrong note in a piece of music, the discordant sound jarring, off-putting. 'Point taken,' he said with a wry smile. 'Is there anyone on your books who you think would be interested in the post?'

Emmie gave a snort of laughter. 'The post? You're making it sound like a job.'

'But it is.'

'It should be a partnership, not a posting.'

'Under normal circumstances, that may well be true, but nothing about my situation is normal,' Matteo said, trying to suppress the desire to grind his teeth. 'I have no desire to marry or have children. My father knew that, and adding that ridiculous codicil to his will was his way of trying to control me beyond the grave.'

'What sort of person was he? I mean, were you ever close to him?'

'He was weak.' Matteo pulled up half a block from the restaurant he'd booked and turned off the engine. He turned to look at Emmie and continued. 'He allowed my mother to walk all over him, and when she left him he completely fell apart. He gave her everything she asked for in the divorce, way more than she was entitled to, compromising his own finances in the vain hope she would come back. But of course, she never did. If anything, his pathetic attempt to please her probably drove her further away.'

'Okay, so I get the aversion to marriage thing, but what about kids? Why have you never wanted them?'

Matteo unclipped his seat belt and picked up his phone from the console below the dashboard. He had wanted one child—his tiny son—and yet he had been taken away from him. Poor little Gabriel had not even taken a breath before his life had been cut short. 'We'd better claim our table. It was a late booking, and if we don't show up on time they might give it to someone else.'

It was a paltry excuse for terminating a conversation but he was done with talking about marriage and kids. His wife's and child's deaths were not common knowledge, given they had happened in Italy and not in England, and he wanted to keep it that way. He was an intensely private person, and besides, he hated talking about his failure. He had failed to protect those who'd needed his protection the most. He had failed to love them as they'd deserved to be loved. He had failed as a husband and father and he was not comfortable with the prospect of becoming either again.

But, with his father's will written the way it was, he had no choice. It was marry and produce an heir or lose everything, including the sacred ground on which his wife and tiny son were buried.

A few minutes later Emmie sat opposite Matteo in one of London's top restaurants. Nothing but the best for Matteo Vitale, she mused. But she didn't think he'd chosen this particular restaurant to impress her. He didn't seem the type of man to resort to such tactics but rather a man who enjoyed good food and wine and pleasant surroundings and didn't mind paying well for it.

'Would you like wine?' he asked, looking at

her over the top of the drinks menu, his glasses perched on his nose.

'I'm not a big drinker,' Emmie said. 'But you go ahead.' Ever since her cancer diagnosis, she had avoided anything that might trigger a relapse. She ate as cleanly as possible, tried to keep her stress levels down, exercised gently but regularly and avoided using chemicals or known carcinogens. She knew it was obsessive at times, but the thought of going through another cancer battle was so terrifying, she was prepared to do whatever she could to avoid facing it all again. She had already caused her family so much stress and heartache by becoming ill in the first place. If she didn't take care of herself to the best of her ability now, she might end up inflicting even more pain on those she loved.

Matteo put the drinks menu down, a wry twist on his mouth. 'I suppose it helps to get your clients drinking so you can draw out their secrets, *si*? *In vino veritas.*'

'In wine lies the truth.' Emmie gave an answering smile. 'Sometimes it helps but I rely on other tactics.'

'Such as?'

She held his penetrating gaze, her heart giving a pony kick against her breast bone. He had such beautiful eyes, she could so easily drown in their bottomless depths. Mysterious, with shifting shadows that intrigued and fascinated her in equal measure. 'I can tell a lot about people by how they move their bodies, what amount of eye contact they're comfortable with, whether they smile a lot or rarely, whether they talk more than they listen—all sorts of stuff.'

'And what is your assessment of me so far?'

'You're not the easiest person to read but I think you're unhappy.'

He gave a bark of humourless laughter. 'I've not long buried my father, so that's hardly a surprising observation.'

'Maybe, but you said you weren't close to him.'

Something flickered through his gaze like a breath of wind across the surface of a deep mountain tarn. His mouth tightened just a fraction and a tiny muscle pulled tighter in the lower quadrant of his lean jaw. 'I'm not happy with how his will is written, that's all.'

'Did you love him?'

He flattened his lips and moved them from side to side, as if deciding whether to respond. After a moment, he let out a short breath. 'I loved him but I didn't respect him for some of the choices he made with his life. He refused to move on from the divorce. To my knowledge, he never had a relationship with another woman. He neglected his duty as a father and as an employer. He allowed the family estate to fall into ruin. It took millions of euros to restore it to what it is today.'

'Your money?' Emmie guessed.

Matteo heaved out another sigh. 'I was happy to pay for everything. If only it would have made him take back control of his life, but no, it was as if he wanted to hurry up his death.'

'What did he die of?'

'Cancer.'

Emmie suppressed a shudder. The *C* word, even after all these years, still triggered her. Memories rushed into her mind of the follow-up appointment a biopsy of her lymph nodes. The doctor's blunt way of delivering the news, her parents' shock and her own fear at what lay ahead. The gruelling chemo regime that had worked for a time, sending her into remission, only for the cancer to flare up again. And again. And again. Months and months of her life locked away in hospital, unable to see her friends in case of infection. Unable to live a normal life for so long, she'd felt like a pariah when she'd finally been released from hospital.

She'd been out of step with her peers. They had all moved on, had finished their education while she had been having toxic chemicals infused through her veins to try and beat the cancer. The shadow of cancer followed her to this day. There was no certainty it wouldn't reoccur. In fact, there was an increased risk she could acquire other cancers as a result of having had Hodgkin's.

And then she had received the most devastating news of all. The high price of saving her life was she would never give life to a baby of her own.

Emmie pushed her gaze up to meet his, hoping he couldn't see any of her inner turmoil. 'What type of cancer?'

'Lung. He smoked even though his doctors were at him for years to give it up.' Matteo's mouth twisted again. 'I know it's an addiction, and a hard one to overcome but there's so much help available these days. He just didn't want to try.'

'It must have been so frustrating for you, watching him slowly kill himself.'

Matteo picked up the food menu. 'Let's talk

about something else. What do you like to eat? The seafood is excellent here.'

Emmie busied herself with studying the menu, but she was just as busy covertly studying him. Like a lot of people, he changed the subject when things got uncomfortable. Clearly talking about his father frustrated and upset him. Watching a parent slowly destroy themselves would have been incredibly painful to watch, and would have made him feel out of control.

She had watched her sister Natalie do much the same thing as his father had, denying her body the food it craved to sustain life, becoming so ill she'd had to be hospitalised time and time again. Emmie had watched on in despair, feeling out of control, unable to help, feeling powerless and useless, and also feeling partly to blame for her sister's illness. Her battle with cancer had consumed her parents' time and energy and then, with their divorce, poor Natty had been pushed to one side, almost becoming invisible as the doctors had fought to save Emmie and her parents and their lawyers had fought over assets and custody arrangements.

Emmie was starting to realise how much control was also incredibly important to Matteo Vitale. It was deeply rooted in his character.

That was why the sudden change to his father's will would have been so terribly shocking. He hadn't been expecting such a thing to occur, especially a condition attached that involved him doing something he clearly had no desire to do—marry and have a child. Lots of men of his age were not ready to settle down but when the right woman came along were more than happy to do so. And Emmie's job was to find the right one for him. But how hard was that going to be when he was not looking for love and all of her clients were?

The waiter approached to take their order, and a short time later Emmie sat back with her glass of freshly squeezed orange juice. 'So, tell me what you do in your free time.'

Matteo gave a slanted smile, as if the concept of free time was amusing. 'I work.'

'But surely you relax sometimes?'

He gave a one-shoulder shrug and picked up his glass of white wine. 'The work I do is very time consuming. I often have a lot of cases on at once, many of which involve the preparation of court documents. I pride myself on making sure I uncover where any discrepancy or fraudulent behaviour has occurred.'

'It sounds very intense.'

'It is.'

Emmie took a sip of her juice and put it back on the table, flicking him a glance. 'Tell me about your family's estate in Umbria. Why is it so important to you? Apart from the money you've spent on it, I mean.'

There was a slight pause, as if he was carefully rehearsing his answer. A screen came down in his gaze and he put his wine glass down with almost exaggerated precision. 'Generations of my family have lived and worked there. I owe it to them to keep it going for generations to come.'

But how would those generations come about if Matteo was so against settling down and having a family? It didn't make sense. If Matteo loved the place so much and wanted it to continue being in the family, surely, he would have considered marrying and producing an heir without having to be forced to do so?

'Presumably that was your father's plan, then, to ensure there was a generation after you. I mean, given you were so against marrying and having a family,' Emmie pointed out.

Matteo frowned so heavily the pleat between his eyebrows could have held a pencil. His hand tensed where it was resting on the table, the fingers opening and closing repeatedly. 'My father could have left it to one of my cousins but he added another condition—if I don't fulfil the terms of his will, the estate can only be sold to someone not connected in any way to the Vitale family.' His hand clenched into a tight fist. 'It was his way of ensuring I did what he wanted. He knew I would never allow it to be sold to a stranger. Someone who might turn it into a hotel or something.'

Emmie chewed her lip, wondering why his father had felt he had to go to such lengths to get Matteo to do as he wished. But she knew all about difficult fathers and the lengths they went to in order to get their way. 'Manipulation is a cruel tactic some parents use to get what they want.'

'That sounds like the voice of experience.' His gentle tone was disarming, so too his unwavering gaze.

She gave a rueful twist of a smile. 'My parents divorced when I was in my late teens. My dad was like a spoilt child who couldn't get his way.' She sighed and added, 'It made a bad situation so much worse.' Emmie was a little shocked she had disclosed to him—a client—such personal information about herself. She normally kept her own issues out of the conversation with clients. Her mission was to get to know him, not have him get to know her.

'Is that why you're not interested in finding love yourself? Only for your clients?'

Emmie tore a small piece off the fresh bread roll on her side plate and dipped it in the olive oil and balsamic vinegar in a tiny dish on the table. 'I'm not cynical about love. I believe in it and love to see it happen between my clients and friends. But I'm not sure I'd make a great partner myself. I'm too much of a workaholic.' She popped the morsel of bread in her mouth and chewed and swallowed.

'Why are you so driven?'

Emmie gave a light laugh. 'Interesting question from someone who claims he doesn't know how to relax.'

'Takes one to know one.' His lazy smile made something in her stomach swoop.

She lowered her gaze from his, her cheeks suddenly warm enough to toast the rest of the bread roll on her plate. After a moment, she looked up to find him watching her with an inscrutable expression. Her breath caught, her heart tripped and her stomach nosedived again. She hastily pulled herself back into line. She was acting like a fool, getting all het up over being in his company. She'd had dinner with loads of clients and had never felt so undone before. Her job was to find out everything she could about him so she could find him a suitable partner. 'Where do you live in Italy? At your family estate or somewhere else?'

'I have apartments in Rome and Milan but I spend most of my time at the estate.'

'Is that where your father lived too?'

'No. He lived in an apartment in Florence to be closer to health services, but retained ownership of the estate.' A ripple of tension travelled across his features. 'He always assured me it would pass to me. I had no reason to doubt him.'

'Did you think of challenging the will? I mean, was he in sound mind when he made the change to it? Maybe if you could prove he wasn't, then you'd have a chance of—'

'I've wasted enough time already trying to challenge it,' Matteo said. 'It's iron-clad and I have no choice but to do as it states. He might have been dying of cancer, but he was in full control of his mind right up to the last. All of his doctors confirmed it.'

Emmie wondered how far the apple had fallen from the tree. The stubborn determination of his father to achieve his goal beyond the grave was reflected in Matteo's grim determination to do whatever he could to secure the estate—even something he clearly didn't want to do. 'Would you be open to having me visit you at the estate at some point?'

'Is that what you would normally do? Travel abroad to visit a client's family home?'

'Sometimes. It depends.'

'On what?'

'On whether I think it will help me to get to know a client better,' Emmie said. 'Would you be agreeable? I know you're a busy man and all, and it's terribly short notice, but you're in a hurry to find a wife and I want to make sure I give you the top-level service you're paying for.'

'How long would you want to stay?' There was a guardedness about his tone that made her wonder if she had overstepped the mark. But she felt compelled to see him at his estate. It was the reason he was so intent on finding a wife to fulfil the terms of his father's will. She refused to acknowledge she had any other reason for wanting to spend more time in his company.

'Two or three days should be enough.'

'I'll see what I can do.'

Emmie smiled. 'Great. I'll get my secretary to clear my diary once you let me know which days suit you. But in the meantime, I'll go through the list of clients on my books to see if there is someone who might suit your requirements.' But, right at that moment, she couldn't think of a single one. Which one of her clients would agree to his unusual request?

Matteo continued to hold her gaze for a beat or two but then his eyes drifted to her mouth for a heart-stopping moment. He blinked and then lifted his eyes back to hers, his expression cast in a deep frown. 'You're not worried about spending time alone with a man you've only just met?'

Emmie was worried but not for the reasons he probably thought. It wasn't him she was afraid of—it was herself. She was drawn to him in a way she couldn't explain. He was like a wounded wolf that was hiding its pain in order to survive. How close would he allow her to get to him? How close did she dare get to him? She gave him an arch look. 'Should I be worried?'

His eyes dipped to her mouth for a brief moment before meshing again with hers. 'Not at all.'

Once their meal was over, Matteo walked Emmie back to his car. He was still mulling over her request to visit him at his family estate. It seemed an odd request and yet he had decided against refusing. He was intrigued by her approach to finding him a wife. He was intrigued by her, full-stop. There was something about her that drew her to him in a way few people did. He was a loner, and preferred his own company, and yet he found her company…interesting. Interesting company, but not exactly relaxing, given her propensity to ask questions he would prefer not to answer. But she was only doing her job—the job he was paying her handsomely to do.

Matteo opened the passenger door and Emmie brushed past him to get into the car. He had to drag his eyes away from the slim length of her legs and he had to ignore the delicate waft of her perfume dancing past his nostrils. He had to ignore the quickening of his blood as she flicked her trench coat out of the way of the door and smiled up at him.

'Thank you.'

'You're welcome.'

He walked round the front of the car, got behind the wheel and started the engine, pulling down his seat belt and finding her looking at him with a small frown on her face. 'What's wrong?'

Her frown smoothed away and she gave a quick on-off smile. 'Nothing. I was just wondering if we could do a detour before you take me home.'

'Where to?'

'Do you stay in hotels when you come to London or do you have an apartment here?'

'I have a house. I travel back and forth a lot—I have an office here in London.'

'Can I see it? Your house, I mean. I'll save your office for another time.'

Matteo put the car in gear and frowned. 'Does all this research you do actually work?'

'If you don't want to take me to your home, then don't.'

That was the whole trouble right there in a big, fat crinkly nutshell. He wanted to take her home and see if that rosy pink mouth felt as soft as it looked beneath the pressure of his. He gave himself a mental shake. Emmie was off the market—or so she'd said. 'Fine. I'll take you to see my house but I can't see what the point is. It's just a house I stay in while I work in London.'

'Yes, but it's a house, not an apartment, which tells me a lot about you.'

Matteo harrumphed and pulled out into the street. 'I had no idea I was such an open book.'

'You're not,' Emmie said with another smile. 'But I like nothing better than a challenge.'

'Just as well, because finding me a wife in such a short time frame is going to be one hell of a challenge.'

'You don't think I can do it?'

Matteo clenched his teeth and his hands. 'I'm counting on you to do it.'

CHAPTER THREE

A FEW MINUTES LATER, Matteo parked his car in front of a beautiful, three-storey Victorian house in Chelsea. 'This is my home,' he said, turning off the engine.

Emmie studied the neat exterior, then glanced his way. 'Is it really a home, though, or just a place to sleep at night?'

He met her look with a frown. 'Has anyone ever told you, you ask a lot of questions?'

She gave him a winning smile. 'It's my job.'

He grunted and opened the driver's door and came around to her side of the car. He opened the door for her and she stepped out, taking care not to touch him on the way past. Emmie was determined to keep things professional and impersonal between them. This wasn't a date with a new man—this was a fact-finding mission with a new client. She had a job to do—a challenging job—and she couldn't afford to be distracted by Matteo Vitale's brooding good looks and magnetic mysteriousness of manner.

Matteo led her inside the gorgeously appointed mansion. It had a functional and masculine feel about it but there were softer touches here and there that perfectly balanced the overall look. 'Is there any particular room you'd like to see?' he asked.

'Where do you spend most of your time when you're here? Apart from your bedroom, of course.' Emmie wished she hadn't mentioned his bedroom. She was dying to take a peek at it, but the thought of entering it with him made her feel hot all over. She could only imagine how many women he took in there and made mad passionate love to. Not that she had read anything about him being an out-and-out playboy, but what woman wouldn't want a night in his arms? There was a sensual energy about him that spoke to her body in a way nothing had ever done before. Her awareness of him increased with every moment she spent with him. She could easily have waited for another day to ask to see his home but she had felt compelled to extend the evening with him, to delve a little more deeply into his enigmatic personality.

'I spend most of my time in my study.'

She rolled her eyes. 'I should have known.'

A half-smile flirted with the corners of his mouth. 'Come this way. It's through here.'

Emmie followed him upstairs to a book-shelf-lined room on the second floor. She walked over to the mullioned windows that overlooked a neat garden at the back of the house. The garden was a mostly formal affair, illuminated by subtle lighting set in sandstone flagstones. There was a small water feature in the centre, complete with water lilies floating on the top, that was also illuminated. It looked like a peaceful place to spend a summer evening entertaining friends, or even to sit in quiet reflection on one's own. She suspected Matteo did the latter far more frequently than the former.

Emmie turned back from the window to cast her eyes over the study. There was a large leather-topped desk in dark wood in front of one row of bookshelves, and it had a leather Chesterfield-type chair. A slimline desk-top computer was situated on the desk and a printer set up on a lower shelf of the bookcase that kept them out of sight.

Emmie ran her gaze along the bookshelves to see what sort of books he liked to read.

There were many Italian titles as well as English ones, and numerous financial tomes, including some hefty tax law volumes. There were a few crime fiction novels and biographies and even some art history. Not surprising, given the art work on the walls looked like originals. But there were no personal photographs of friends or family although, given what he'd told her about his parents, that too wasn't all that surprising.

'Seen enough?' Matteo asked.

Emmie turned from examining the bookshelves to face him. 'It's a nice study. It's got an old-world atmosphere, suggesting you're a bit of a traditionalist at heart.'

A cynical light entered his gaze. 'On some issues, perhaps. Others not so much.' He walked over to the door. 'I'll go and put some coffee on and let you have a wander around on your own.'

'Are you sure you'd be comfortable with me doing that?'

'If I find something valuable missing after you leave, I know where to find you.' His tone was playful, his smile teasing, and it made her heart give an extra beat. It was the first full smile he had given her and it transformed his features, making him appear younger and even more attractive.

'I can assure you, I am completely trustworthy.'

'There's nothing here you could steal that couldn't be replaced.'

But what about your heart?

The errant thought shocked Emmie into silence and, within another moment, he had gone.

Matteo went to put on some coffee, wondering if he had made a mistake in engaging Emmie's professional services. Her approach seemed reasonable on one level, but he was uneasy her mission to get to know him might reveal things about himself he would prefer to keep hidden. But any misgivings on his part would have to be shelved—he had to find a wife sooner rather than later. The deadline set out in his father's will was rapidly approaching and, while he could have cast his net via a dating app, he hadn't wanted to risk attracting the wrong person. A professional dating agency, especially one with Emmie Woodcroft's reputation for excellent service and results, was his best option.

What he hadn't expected was Emmie herself to be so alluring. Or so against finding a partner herself. It seemed a little odd for a professional match-maker to be single. After all, she knew how to find the right person for her clients—how much easier to find one for herself? He admired her ambition, the focus on her career, but something about her adamant stance on singledom didn't ring true.

His job was to spot irregularities, to uncover secrets and hidden information. Was there some other reason Emmie wasn't interested in finding love? Had she been hurt in the past? Had her heart broken by a lover? Been frightened off commitment because of the fear of losing herself in a relationship and not being able to follow her dream career the way she wanted to? She certainly put a lot of her time into her clients. Her willingness to travel and spend time individually with them was commendable. It was no wonder she got the results she did. And, as long as she got results for him, he would be happy. Well, as happy as he could be under the circumstances, and as circumstances went they weren't exactly happy-making.

Emmie peeped into a couple of the spare rooms on the upper floor but the one room she was drawn to look at was Matteo's bedroom. She

walked towards it as if pulled by a powerful
magnet and gently pushed the door open. She
stepped over the threshold and breathed in the
light citrussy notes of his aftershave that lin-
gered in the air. The king-sized bed dominated
the room and drew her gaze as if the same
powerful magnet was at work. The bed linen
was a blinding white, but there was a dark-
blue throw on the end of the bed, as well as
three scatter cushions in the same hue propped
against the array of snowy-white pillows. Twin
bedside lamps and tables were at either side of
the bed. The left-side table had a book with a
bookmark poking out of the top, which told her
Matteo slept on the left side of the bed.

She moved across the room and took a peek
in the walk-in wardrobe. His clothes were
neatly organised, even colour coordinated,
which suggested either he was a little pedan-
tic or obsessive or his housekeeper was. She
assumed he had one. The place was immacu-
late and, given he was such a busy man who
travelled a lot for work, she couldn't imagine
him wandering around his many homes flicking a duster over the furniture and doing his
own laundry.

She slid the pocket door closed and went to
have a peek at the *en suite*. It was stylishly and

luxuriously appointed in white Italian marble with veins of grey and black running through. The large shower area triggered her thoughts into imagining him in there naked, hot water from the shower attachment splashing over his toned and hard male flesh. She suppressed a shiver and moved further into the *en suite* and picked up a bottle of his aftershave from the marble counter, unscrewing the cap and holding it up to her nose. It was intoxicating but not half as intoxicating when it was mixed with his own personal scent. She closed her eyes and took another sniff...

'Found anything interesting?' Matteo's deep voice sounding from the *en suite* doorway startled Emmie into dropping the cologne bottle on the marble floor. It smashed into several pieces and she gasped in horror at the mess she'd created.

'I'm so sorry!' She bent down and began to pick up the pieces, but the first shard of glass cut her finger and large droplets of blood began dripping to the floor. *Eek!* How could she have been so clumsy?

'Leave it.' Matteo snatched up a snowy-white hand towel and crouched down beside her, holding her hand and inspecting her finger for fragments of glass before he wrapped her hand in the towel to stem the flow of blood. 'Are you okay?'

Emmie was sure her cheeks were as bright red as the droplets of blood on the floor. Never had she felt so hideously embarrassed. What must he think of her, snooping round his bathroom? She was hardly acting like a consummate professional. She was acting like a star-struck teenager let loose in a celebrity's house, hunting for a souvenir to take home. Seriously, what was wrong with her? She had never acted so out of line before. Never.

'I'm fine. I'm really sorry. You startled me and I… I shouldn't have been snooping around in your bathroom, but I really like your cologne. It's one of the nicest ones I've ever smelt and I…' She scrunched her eyes closed and opened them again to say with a self-conscious grimace, 'I'll shut up now. Nothing I can say can excuse my appalling behaviour. Please forgive me.'

Matteo helped her to her feet, his towering height all the more apparent in comparison to her smaller stature. The top of her head barely came up to his shoulder. He was so close she could feel his body warmth and she had to resist the temptation to move even closer. She hadn't been this close to a man for years. In fact, the only men who had touched her since her teens were her oncologist and the occasional male nurse.

Matteo was still holding her hand wrapped in the towel, his expression etched in lines of concern. 'There's nothing to forgive. I'd better take another look to see if it's stopped bleeding. Do you mind?'

'Go for it.'

He peeled the towel away and inspected the wound with a frown of concentration. The blood was still seeping, so he quickly bound it up again and applied more pressure. 'You're lucky you didn't sever a tendon or something. Does it hurt?'

'Not really.' What hurt was standing so close to him and wanting to lift her face to be kissed. Emmie kept her gaze lowered, worried he might see what she was trying so hard to suppress. The need to be held by him, to feel his arms go around her and bring her closer to the hard, warm frame of his body. It was as if her body was under some weird sort of spell, activated the first moment she'd met him.

'Do you feel light-headed? Faint?' His other hand slipped to her other wrist and measured her pulse. 'Your pulse is quite fast.'

'I—I always have a fast resting pulse. I'm not very…erm…fit…'

His thumb stayed on the blue-veined skin of her wrist, his eyes holding hers in a lock that made her insides twist and coil with lust. 'You don't look unfit to me.' His voice was deep and low with an edge of huskiness. His thumb began to stroke her wrist in a slow caress that sent her pulse rate soaring.

'I—I can't run up a flight of stairs without getting breathless.' Nor could she stand in such close proximity to him without becoming breathless. Breathless with longing, a longing she had never expected to feel with such intensity. A longing she *had* to suppress.

His lazy smile made something in her stomach turn over. His eyes were so dark she could barely make out his pupils from the sea of dark, bottomless blue. His gaze drifted to her mouth and she disguised a swallow…or tried to. The silence was so thick she could hear the up and down movement of her throat and, judging from his expression, so could he. His eyes went to her mouth again, lingering there for an infinitesimal moment.

Emmie didn't realise she was holding her breath until her lungs began to beg for more air. She snatched in a wobbly breath and pulled her hand out of his, holding the towel in place. 'Do you have a bandage I could borrow? I'm really sorry about this. I feel so foolish. I'm not normally so clumsy.'

'Stop apologising. I'm just glad you didn't do any worse damage.' He opened one of the drawers below the marble basins and took out a first aid kit and laid it on the counter. He opened the kit and took out a crepe bandage as well as antiseptic and cotton pads. He turned back to take her hand again, peeling away the towel to check the bleeding. 'We'd better give it a wash under cold water just in case there are any tiny fragments of glass embedded in there.'

'I can't feel any. It's just a clean cut.'

He held her hand under the cold tap and, even though his touch was gentle, it made her intensely aware of every point of contact with her skin as if she was being permanently branded by him. Her arm brushed his shirt sleeve and it was impossible not to notice the firm muscles the fine cotton covered. Her gaze drifted to his hand, holding hers under the water, his skin tanned, his fingers long and strong. She thought of his hands touching her in other places—places that hadn't been touched by a man in so long she had forgotten what it felt like.

She stole a glance at his profile while he was concentrating on cleansing her finger. The dark stubble surrounding his nose and mouth and running over his lean jaw made her want to reach up and stroke her fingers along its sexy roughness. She wondered what it would feel like against her softer skin. Her heartbeat increased as her thoughts ran wild, let out of a locked vault inside her head—thoughts of being kissed by his firm mouth, touched by his surprisingly gentle hands, possessed by his hard maleness. A soft flutter in her feminine core brought forth an involuntary gasp and he glanced at her with an apologetic look.

'Sorry if this stings.' Matteo turned off the water and dried her hand with a fresh towel and then proceeded to dab the wound with antiseptic.

'I've felt worse pain.'

He gave her another sideways glance as if something in her tone intrigued him. 'A broken bone?'

'No, just the usual cuts and bruises.'

Matteo continued to dress her wound and finished up with winding a bandage around her finger, padding it with cotton wool beneath to protect it from bumping. She found herself wishing she had a bigger wound so she could stay close to him longer. 'There you go.'

'You missed your calling as a doctor.'

He gave a soft laugh, which was even more breath-snatching than his smile. 'My bedside manner would need some work.'

'I don't know about that.'

His eyes met hers and time seemed to come to a standstill. The silence was so thick she could feel it pressing from all four corners of the room. Emmie could feel the colour pouring back into her cheeks and sank her teeth into her lower lip. 'I think I need to go home now. It's way past my bedtime.' Oh, dear God, could she just stop mentioning the word *bed*?

Matteo guided her out of the *en suite* with a gentle hand at her elbow. 'Careful—there's still glass on the floor.'

'I'll replace the bottle of cologne for you.'

'Don't be silly.'

'I insist.' Emmie moved away to put some distance between them before she made an even bigger fool of herself. 'And I'll catch a cab home. I've taken up too much of your time.'

'I'll take you home, and that's not negotiable. Understood?' He had an intractable light in his eyes that should have annoyed her but somehow didn't. She was looking forward to eking out the last few minutes of the evening in his company before the clock struck midnight.

Cinderella has nothing on me, Emmie thought. Just as well she wasn't wearing glass slippers or she would likely shatter them too.

Matteo pulled up in front of Emmie's house a few minutes later. He was out of the car and round to open her door before she had even undone her seat belt. Emmie stepped out onto the footpath and turned to face him. 'Thank you for dinner.'

'I'll walk you to your door.'

'I'm sure I won't sever an artery between here and my front door,' Emmie said with a self-deprecating smile.

Something flickered in his gaze and his lower jaw tightened. 'You should probably get a doctor to check your finger in the morning. It could become infected.' He placed a gentle hand below her elbow and guided her towards her door.

Emmie had so rarely been touched by a man she decided that was why Matteo's touch was doing such weird things to her. In fact, she couldn't recall the last time a man had got close to her, held her, kissed her, looked at her with desire gleaming in his eyes. Matteo's eyes were inscrutable most of the time but every now and again she caught a glimpse of something that looked like interest. The same interest she was trying so hard not to show in her own gaze.

Emmie took out her key from her bag but realised her cut finger was going to make unlocking the door difficult. But Matteo had already anticipated that and held out his hand for her key. 'I'll do it.' She slipped the key into the broad span of his palm but somehow her fingers brushed against his skin and a flicker of electricity shot through her body.

Matteo unlocked the door and pushed it open for her. 'There you go.' He handed her the key but it was impossible to take it without touching him again. The lightning bolt of awareness zapped from her fingers to her armpit and all the way down to her core like the fizzing wick of a firework.

Emmie closed her hand around her key and stepped across the threshold but then turned and faced him. 'Would you like to come in?' She issued the invitation before her rational mind caught up and warned her against spending any more time alone with him.

His dark eyebrows rose ever so slightly

above his unreadable eyes, the only sign her invitation had surprised him. 'Sure.' He stepped through the door and closed it with a soft click behind him.

Emmie ran the tip of her tongue across her lips, her breath stalling when his gaze followed the movement.

'Erm, would you like a drink? Cocoa? Hot chocolate? Juice? I'm afraid I don't have any alcohol.' She knew she sounded as unsophisticated as she felt. She was offering him nursery-school drink options when no doubt he was used to complicated cocktails and nifty little nightcaps.

One side of his mouth came up in a half-smile. 'It's actually nice to meet someone who doesn't drink.'

'Would you like me to add that to your list of requirements in a partner?' Emmie asked.

'A moderate drinker is fine.'

Emmie turned away to hang her coat on the coat stand near the door. 'I guess your future wife will have to give up drinking anyway if she's to become pregnant as soon as possible.' Even saying the word made her heart ache for what she could never have. She imagined him holding a new-born baby. Somehow, she knew he would be an excellent father. Strong, dependable, protective.

'Yes.'

Emmie turned to face him again, not entirely confident her features were as neutral as she would have liked. 'But what if she doesn't get pregnant straight away? Some couples take many months to fall pregnant. Sometimes years. And others, never.'

'And others on their first attempt.' His expression was shuttered but his tone contained a note of something she couldn't quite identify. It sounded cynical and yet it had an undertone of something else.

Emmie searched his face for a clue but it was like trying to read a marble bust. 'I guess that would be ideal for your situation, but you can't guarantee it will happen.'

'It has to happen, otherwise I stand to lose everything I've worked so hard to keep.' The implacable quality to his voice was a reminder of his determined nature. Once he set his mind to something, he would not stop until he achieved it. But some things in life were impossible to achieve no matter how much you wanted them. She, of all people, knew that only too well.

'I have women on my books who desperately want to have a family, but they also want love,' Emmie said. 'And therein lies the problem, because you want the former but not the latter.'

'It's my experience that if you pay someone enough they will agree to whatever you want them to do.' There was no doubt about the cynicism in his tone now. Every word positively dripped with it.

Emmie gave him a tight smile. 'You're going to be a hard sell, Mr Vitale, but never let it be said I baulk at a challenge.'

Matteo held her gaze for a beat longer than she was comfortable with but she was determined not to look away first. His gaze drifted to her mouth and she had to resist the urge to moisten her lips. 'Do you live alone?' His gaze came back to hers and she could feel her cheeks heating.

'Yes.'

He cast his gaze around the spacious interior. 'It's a big house for one person.'

'I like my own space.'

'Fair enough.' He studied her for a long moment, his eyes moving over every inch of her face, as if searching for something. Emmie kept as still as she possibly could, barely taking a breath in case she betrayed how unsettled she was in his disturbing company. Not creepily disturbing, but disturbing to her sense of equilibrium. Everything about him made her feel on edge, worried he would see more than she wanted him to see.

'You're a very unusual young woman, Emmie.' His voice dropped to a low burr that reminded her of distant thunder. Nature signalling a warning of approaching danger. Danger that could upend her carefully ordered life and make her want things she had no business wanting.

Emmie glanced at the shape of his mouth and imagined it pressed to her own. Those firm, determined lips moving against hers, drawing from her a fervent response that she sensed would set fire to every cell in her body. She drew in a prickly breath and took an unsteady step backwards, and would have stumbled if not for the quick action of his hand coming out to stabilise her.

'Are you okay?' His brows snapped together in concern, his grip gentle but firm, his touch sending waves of awareness rippling through her body.

Not in your presence, I'm not. But she could hardly say it out loud.

'I—I'm fine.' Emmie pasted a bright smile on her mouth.

His gaze lowered to her mouth, his hand on her arm moving to press ever so gently on the small of her back, bringing her slowly, inexorably closer to the warm, male heat of his body. There was a dark intensity in his hooded gaze and her blood quickened, as if suddenly injected with a potent drug. A drug that pushed aside her normal inhibitions and sent her senses spinning out of control.

Emmie licked her lower lip, breathing in the intimate warmth of his breath that danced over hers, her eyes lowering to half-mast. She was drugged, dazed, dazzled by the ever-so-slow descent of his mouth, her breath hitching in the nanosecond before he touched down. His lips were firm and yet soft, moving against hers in a languid manner, exploring the landscape of her lips before lazily stroking the seam of her mouth with his tongue. A hot shiver coursed down her spine and Emmie parted her lips on a gasp of pleasure, hungrily responding to his erotic entry, the very hairs on her head standing up at the roots in sensual delight.

Emmie murmured against his lips, wanting more, needing more. But then a voice sounded in her head, reminding her of the danger she would drift into by becoming involved with Matteo. He was not just a healthy man in his prime but more importantly a client. What was she thinking? It was completely and utterly unprofessional. She had never crossed such an important line before, nor had she ever been tempted to do so.

With what little self-control she had left, she pulled away from him, her cheeks warm, her lips hotter from where his had pressed so expertly, so temptingly. 'Erm, I'm sorry. I—I don't want you to think I allow all my male clients to kiss me. I don't know how or why that happened, but it must *not* happen again.' She straightened her shoulders and painted on a formal expression. 'Now, about that drink?'

A crooked smile formed on his lips, his eyes glinting. 'Let's leave it for another time.'

It? What 'it' was he referring to? A drink or something even more potent to her senses? 'I guess hot chocolate or fruit juice isn't quite up to your sophisticated taste?' Emmie put in with an attempt at an I'm-not-flustered-by-you-one-little-bit smile.

'It's late and I should let you get to bed. We both have to work tomorrow.'

There was the 'bed' word again, and some-how hearing it from his lips made it even worse. Especially when she could still taste his lips on her own. Her mind conjured up images of her in bed with him, their limbs entangled, their naked bodies pressed together in the throes of passionate sex.

Emmie had never had passionate sex, only a teenage fumble and the hit-and-miss sort of mild pleasure that had left her disappointed and wondering what all the fuss was about. She hadn't been brave enough to have sex since her diagnosis and treatment. Sharing her body with someone post-cancer was too confronting. But, now that Matteo had kissed her, she was tempted in a way she had never been tempted before to experience competent lovemaking. To lie in a man's arms and be pleasured like she had never been pleasured before. For his lovemaking would be nothing if not competent, she was sure. Matteo Vitale had an aura of sexual competence about him and it called out to every hungry cell in her body.

But she could not be tempted. Must *not* be tempted again. It was completely unprofessional and would only waste valuable time for him to achieve his goal.

Emmie quickly did a mental scan of her clients and came up with a name. Karena Thorsby wasn't a perfect fit for him but she came reasonably close. 'Look, speaking of work, I wonder if I do have someone who might suit your requirements. Would you be interested in meeting her for a drink, perhaps tomorrow if I can arrange it? If she suits, I wouldn't need to come to Umbria after all. I mean, it will save time for you, not to mention money.'

Matteo's gaze held hers in a lock that made the backs of her knees tingle. His expression was impossible to read and it made her all the more determined to keep her distance. She had never met anyone so intriguing, so alluring and complex. So dangerously tempting.

'Fine. I'll clear my diary.'

Emmie licked her lips and was shocked at how sensitive they still were, as if his kiss had somehow changed them. Charging them with such sensual energy they could never be the same.

'So, I'll be in touch as soon as I speak to Karena.' She moved towards the front door, desperate to get him to leave before she changed her mind. She opened the door and stretched her lips into another forced smile. 'Thank you again for dinner and for the lift home.'

Matteo stood in the frame of the doorway and looked down at her with his inscrutable expression still in place. His eyes briefly dipped to her mouth before coming back to hold hers. 'Goodnight.'

Emmie was aware of every thudding beat of her heart, aware of the hum of sensual energy in the air passing from his body to hers, aware of the magnetic pull of his gaze. Aware of the silent throb of blood still coursing through her kiss-swollen lips. ''Night.'

She closed the door once he'd left, and leaned back against it and let out a long, serrated sigh. 'Don't even think about it.' She whispered the words but they rang in the silence like a clanging alarm bell.

CHAPTER FOUR

MATTEO SUPPRESSED YET another yawn as Karena Thorsby told him her sad relationship history and why she was now thirty-four and desperate to settle down and make babies with the man of her dreams. But, while he conceded that she was attractive and intelligent, and had every right to want to fulfil her dream of happy-ever-after, he'd known from the moment he met her he wasn't the one to give it to her. There was no chemistry, no electric spark, no longing on his part to see her again.

Unlike with Emmie Woodcroft.

Every time he thought of Emmie, he thought of her periwinkle-blue eyes and lush mouth. The sweet softness of her lips and how they had clung to his when he'd kissed her. He thought of her petite frame pressed closely to his as he'd attended to her cut finger. How soft her skin was, how small her hand in comparison to his. He recalled the fragrance of her, the geranium and bergamot scent that was as intoxicating as a drug.

From the moment he'd met her, he had been drawn to her in a way he had never experienced with anyone else. Of course, he had felt instant desire in the past, but somehow with Emmie it went further than primal urges. Way, way further. It was as if she had some other indefinable element to her personality that called out to his on a silent radar frequency that sent tingles dancing along his flesh.

Finally, his date with Karena finally ended, his only comfort being she didn't seem all that disappointed, or even surprised, when he said he wasn't interested in repeating it.

He drove home with his mind replaying his dinner date with Emmie—how he had been disappointed when the evening had finally come to an end. He let out a sigh and turned his car into his street. Was he strangely fixated on Emmie because she had made it clear she wasn't interested in finding a partner? Did his male ego see her as some sort of fresh challenge? He usually had no trouble finding casual partners, but right now he wasn't after a fling. He needed a wife in a hurry, and obsessing about a young woman who had no plans to marry any time soon, if ever, would only waste his valuable time.

And yet, that kiss between them had shown him she was as drawn to him as he was to her.

Could he get Emmie to change her mind?

Emmie caught up with Karena the following day when she popped into Emmie's office on her lunch break.

'So, how did your date with Matteo Vitale go?'

Karena plonked herself down in the chair opposite Emmie's desk. 'Don't get me wrong, he was polite and easy on the eye, but I didn't feel any connection with him at all. In fact, I found him a little intimidating—more than a little, if I'm honest. I kept babbling on to fill the awkward silences but I think he was bored the whole time we were together.'

Emmie should have felt disappointed it hadn't worked out for Matteo with Karena but strangely she was not. Nor was she going to examine too closely why she wasn't disappointed. 'I'm sorry. I guess he can be a little intimidating when you first meet him. But I do have another client who might be better for you. I've only just finished entering his details into the system.'

She clicked on her computer screen and scrolled through the list till she came to a divorced man of a similar age to Karena. 'Colin Appleby is looking for all the things you are. His wife left him a couple of years ago because he wanted children and she didn't. I'll organise a meeting for you both if you like?'

'Please do. My biological clock is ticking so loudly, it keeps me awake at night.'

Emmie forced her lips into an empathetic smile, her heart twisting into a tight knot in her chest. 'I can only imagine how awful that must be but let's hope Colin is The One.'

Karena had only been gone half an hour when Paisley informed her she had another visitor. 'It's Mr Vitale,' she said in a stage whisper. 'He's insisting on seeing you now. He's making rather a habit of this, isn't he? Shall I insist on him making an appointment or send him in?'

Emmie tried to ignore the soft flutter around her heart and rose from her chair. She suspected anyone insisting that Matteo Vitale do anything would be an impossible task. He had an iron will and a steely resolve that would daunt most people. But she was not most people and, besides, he was paying her a large sum of money, so she had to make his needs a priority. 'Send him in.' She smoothed her hands down the sides of her skirt, her pulse already picking up its pace.

Matteo came in looking as dashingly handsome as ever, especially with his windblown hair, and dressed in a dark suit the same colour as his eyes. He looked like a brooding hero from a Gothic romance, the landscape of his face drawn into harsh lines, his unusually blue eyes as dark as a midnight sky.

'Really? Was that the best you could do?' His blunt question was delivered with a cutting note of disdain.

Emmie refused to be intimidated by him, somehow understanding his natural inclination was to push people away rather than draw them near. 'Look, these things take time and—'

'I don't have time. I'm paying you a truckload of money to find me a wife, but if you can't find someone even remotely suitable then please tell me now so I can make other arrangements.'

'I'm working on it. Please, take a seat. Paisley has organised my travel arrangements and I can be in Umbria next week. Spending time with you will give me a clearer idea of—'

'Next week?' His eyes flashed with impatience and he remained standing, his imposing height never more apparent. 'Why not this weekend?'

Emmie disguised a convulsive swallow. She needed time to prepare herself, to get her head round spending an extended period of time with him. That impulsive kiss between them at her house warned her of the danger in being alone with him. She took a calming breath and straightened her spine, eyeballing him as if she was a stern schoolmistress dressing down a recalcitrant student.

'Mr Vitale, it no longer surprises me you've found it hard to find a suitable partner. I understand you like things done quickly, but I can't just shuffle around my diary to suit you. I have other clients to see to.'

'You have staff, don't you? Get them to see to them.'

Emmie gave him a look so glacial she fully expected the glass of water on her desk to freeze on the spot. 'You know, you might have had a chance with Karena if you hadn't scared the hell out of her. You made her nervous.'

'She should be an anaesthetist,' he shot back, scraping a hand through his already tousled hair. 'She would save the NHS a fortune on drugs. I swear to God, she almost put me to sleep by telling me about every man she'd ever dated and why they hadn't worked out.' He dropped his hand by his side and continued in a less harsh tone, 'Not that she wasn't a nice person, but she's far from my type.'

'Ah yes, your type,' Emmie said with an arch look. 'And that type would be...?'

He held her gaze for a throbbing moment, his eyes so dark and unreadable her heart skipped a beat. 'The type of woman who would agree to marry me for a year or two, max, and provide me with an heir.'

'But what sort of woman do you normally date?'

'The no-strings type.'

'It's my experience there are a lot less of them around than most men think,' Emmie said. 'Relationships, even casual ones, rarely come without strings, or indeed consequences. Someone nearly always gets hurt.'

Matteo drew in a deep breath and turned away to go and stand in front of her window, looking at the sliver of a view she paid a fortune in rent to stand on tiptoe and crane her neck to see. One of his hands came up to rub at the back of his neck as if to loosen a knot of tension. He rolled his shoulders and released a long sigh, turning around to look at her. 'It's never been my intention to hurt anyone, but yes, it has happened in the past.'

'Have you ever fallen in love?'

'No.'

'But someone did with you?'

A flicker of pain passed through his gaze. 'Unfortunately, yes.'

'Unfortunately, because…?'

'We were totally unsuitable for each other.' His tone was flat, his expression bleak. 'You have no idea of the pain I caused and there's nothing I can do to change a damn thing about it. Not now.'

Emmie came round from behind her desk and laid a gentle hand on his forearm. 'Do you want to talk about it?' She kept her voice soft, her gaze searching his pained one.

He blinked as if to recalibrate his mood and his expression became shuttered. 'No. Talking about it won't change a thing.' His hand came down over the top of hers and a frisson passed through her body. At first, she thought he was going to remove her hand from his arm, but he seemed to change his mind and took her hand in his. His long, tanned fingers curled around hers and he began to stroke the fleshy part at the base of her thumb, his gaze locking on hers. 'You're good at this.'

'At what?'

'Finding out people's darkest secrets.'

'But you're determined not to tell me yours.'

His eyes went to her mouth for a heart-stopping moment. Was he recalling their stolen kiss? The heat of it, the warm press of flesh on flesh, the erotic tangle their tongues? 'Doesn't everyone have something they would rather keep private?' His gaze locked back on hers and a tiny shiver raced across her scalp.

Emmie looked down at their joined hands, her stomach swooping at the sight of his tanned skin against her lighter skin. 'Maybe.'

Matteo turned over her hand and inspected the bandage on her finger. 'How is it feeling?'

'It's fine. Oh, that reminds me…' She pulled her hand out of his and went back to her desk and opened the top drawer on the left side. She took out the bottle of cologne she'd bought to replace the one she had broken at his house and came back to him with it. 'For you.'

He took the cologne with a lopsided smile. 'You didn't need to do that.'

'Yes, I did. I still feel embarrassed about that night.' And not just about the broken bottle. The kiss. She had relived that kiss so many times since.

'Don't be. I can see you have an inquisitive nature.'

Emmie gave a rueful smile. 'That's a polite way of saying I'm a nosy busybody.'

He gave an answering smile that sent a warm flutter through her lower body. He passed the bottle of cologne from one hand to the other, his eyes still holding hers. 'I'll pay you double to come to Umbria this weekend.'

Emmie spluttered out a shocked laugh. 'Don't be ridiculous. You don't have to bribe me. I'll come. But I insist on making my own way there.'

'Fine.' He held the cologne bottle in his right hand and, taking a piece of paper off a sticky note pad on her desk, took a pen out of his jacket pocket, wrote down an address and handed it to her. 'I'll look forward to seeing you there.'

So will I, Emmie thought. Way more than she had any right to.

Emmie drove the hire car through the stone and wrought-iron entrance to Matteo's Umbrian estate. She had insisted on making her own way to Italy, wanting to maintain some independence rather than relying totally on him. The long driveway was lined on either side by rows and rows of lush grape vines, and on the slopes in the distance was an expansive olive grove. There were woods on another side of the property, and a lake, as well as a small river, with a stone bridge across it that led to the villa at the top of a steep hill.

Emmie could immediately see why Matteo was so keen to keep possession of the estate. The villa was centuries old but in wonderful condition with beautiful gardens, both formal and informal. The stunning view from the top of the hill where the villa was situated was enough to steal anyone's breath away, and she was no exception. Emmie turned off the engine and got out of the car and stood for a long moment, looking out over acres and acres of verdant land, imagining Matteo's ancestors tilling the soil. The sun shone down on her with delicious warmth, birds tweeting in the nearby shrubbery, the leaves of the trees rustling in the light summer breeze.

She shaded her eyes from the bright sun with one hand, then turned and caught a glimpse of Matteo coming towards her dressed in nothing but dark blue denim jeans and brown leather work boots. His hair was tousled by the breeze, and his broad, tanned chest shone with perspiration, and Emmie had never seen him look more heart-stoppingly attractive.

'You're early,' Matteo said, roughly finger-combing his hair.

'I—I was bumped forward to an earlier flight.' Emmie felt strangely shy and tongue-tied. 'And it didn't take me as long as I thought to find my way here.'

'I'll get one of the staff to get your luggage. Come inside out of the sun. You already look flushed from the heat.'

Emmie was flushed because seeing his toned chest and abdomen was doing serious damage to her heart rate. Coils of tight muscles rippled from his chest to the waist band of his jeans and her imagination did the rest as to what was below. 'It is a lot hotter than I expected.' And so was he. She had already suspected he had a good body underneath the designer suits he wore but not as breath-catching as this. Her fingers twitched, tempted to reach out and stroke his abdomen to see if it was as rock-hard as it looked.

'If you have staff, why are you working in the fields?' Emmie asked on their way to the villa's entrance.

'My job as a forensic accountant is a desk job with long periods of sitting. I like the exercise working on the estate, not to mention the fresh air.'

Emmie turned and looked at the view again before he caught her staring at his toned body. 'It's beautiful, Matteo. I can see why you love it so much and want to keep it in your possession. If I lived here, I would never want to leave.'

There was a funny little silence only broken by the whistling of the breeze and the twittering birds.

Emmie turned to look at him to find him looking at her with a frown. 'Is something wrong?' she asked.

Matteo gave a movement of his lips that was just shy of a smile. 'I need to take a shower before I give you the grand tour. I'll get my housekeeper, Valentina, to take you to your room and give you some refreshments.'

'Oh, lovely, I could do with a nice cup of tea.'

A short time later, Emmie was led upstairs to a beautifully decorated guest room on the second storey by the housekeeper, who unfortunately didn't speak much English. Emmie had to resort to sign language, as her smattering of Italian didn't extend much besides greetings and 'please' and 'thank you.' It was frustrating, because she had hoped to find out what she could about Matteo via his staff. How someone behaved as an employer was often a clue to how they behaved in other contexts. But, even without the benefit of talking to Valentina, Emmie could see the older woman adored him. Her black-button eyes all but sparkled whenever she mentioned his name.

Once Valentina had left, Emmie finished her refreshing cup of tea and then freshened up. The view from the window in her room drew her back yet again to gaze at the rolling fields and dense woods in the background. She was not a city girl at heart, and had spent most of her childhood in Devon three and a half hours from London in a small village. But her cancer diagnosis and subsequent treatment—not to mention travelling back and forth, overnight accommodation and other expenses— had made it impossible for her parents to keep up with the mortgage payments, so their lovely little country property had had to be sold.

It had been yet another casualty of her illness, one she found hard to forgive herself for, even though she knew on an intellectual level the cancer hadn't been her fault. But in her heart, she still ached for what her illness had done to her family. No one had escaped the fallout and each in their own way was still paying the price.

There was a firm knock on the door and Emmie turned from the window. 'Come in.'

Matteo entered the room and her heart stumbled. He was freshly showered, his hair still damp and curling where it brushed the collar of his casual, open-necked white shirt. He had changed into navy chinos and black leather boots and, even though he was a couple of metres from her, she could pick up the citrus notes of his aftershave. Seriously, she was becoming addicted to that smell. She'd been tempted to buy two bottles when she'd bought the replacement bottle for him. One for him and one for her to sniff in private like a forbidden drug.

'All settled in?' Matteo asked.

'Yes, thank you. But I'm not sure I was able to communicate how happy I was with the room to Valentina. I'm afraid my Italian is a bit patchy.'

'I'll pass on your appreciation.'

'How long has she worked for you?'

'Fifteen years.'

'That's nice.' Emmie moved from the window to tidy the tea things on the tray the housekeeper had left, more to do something with her hands. Being in a bedroom with Matteo Vitale was having a potent effect on her, one she had to do her best to control. 'It shows you're a good employer.'

'But it also could be the money I pay her, *si*?'

Emmie shifted her lips from side to side, her arms crossed against her body, and studied his cynical expression for a moment. 'You don't think much of my powers of observation, do you?'

He came closer to stand within touching distance and she had to work hard to keep her breathing under control. 'Body language is not fool proof, and people's motivations can be easily disguised.' His voice was deep and rough and sent a shiver cascading down her spine. 'Like yours, for instance.'

'M-mine?' Her voice barely got above a cracked whisper and her pulse began to race. She was conscious of how close he was, the heat of his body stirring hers into a frenzy of want. She had to crane her neck to maintain eye contact but every now and again, as if of their own volition, her eyes flicked to his mouth. And, before she could stop the impulse, the point of her tongue came out and licked across her lips.

Matteo placed a gentle hand beneath her

chin, his touch light but electric. Lightning bolts of awareness shot through her entire body and a liquid pool of longing stirred deep and low in her core. His eyes were as dark as midnight, moving between hers in a back and forth motion before becoming hooded and lowering to her mouth. 'Why are you so keen on finding a happy-ever-after for other people but not for yourself?'

Emmie called on every bit of willpower she possessed to step out of his light hold. She wrapped her arms even tighter around her body and moved so the bed was between then. *Oh, dear Lord, the bed.* It seemed to dominate the room. It seemed to be all she thought about—a bed with he and her in it, making mad, passionate love. 'I could ask why you find it so satisfying being a forensic accountant,' she threw back.

'I like righting wrongs.'

'And I like making people happy.'

He gave a slanted smile that didn't reach his eyes. 'But, sadly, that is not always possible. Some people can never be made happy.'

Emmie moved away from the bed and back to the window, adopting a casual pose against the windowsill she was far from feeling. 'Perhaps they feel they don't deserve to be happy.'

He gave a loose-shouldered shrug, his expression equally noncommittal. 'You're an idealist, I'm a realist. We don't speak the same language.'

'I'm an optimist and you're cynical, but that's understandable given how your mother left so early in your life,' Emmie said. 'You have attachment issues. You will never be happy with anyone until you address your fear of intimacy.'

Matteo came to join her at the window, standing so close to her she could see the dark points of stubble along his jaw. He lifted his hand to her face, trailing an idle finger down the curve of her cheek, from her ear to her chin, and every nerve in her face rioted in tingling pleasure. 'Ah, but is it me with the fear of intimacy or you, hmm?' His tone was gently teasing, his touch spine-loosening, his proximity spellbinding.

Emmie sucked in a breath, her heart threatening to beat its way out of her chest. She couldn't stop staring at his mouth, drawn to its sensual contours by a force as old as time. Her lower body began to throb with a primal beat of blood, swelling sensitive tissues, sending tingles and darts and arrows of greedy want through her flesh.

'I— It depends what you mean by intimacy.' She was annoyed her voice wasn't as steady as she would have liked. 'Anyone can jump into bed and have sex, even perfect strangers. True intimacy is much more than that.'

His thumb began a rhythmical stroke of her cheek, like a metronome arm set on the slowest possible time signature. 'Who is the person you are closest to?' His hand paused its stroking, as if waiting for her to answer.

Emmie looked at him blankly for a moment, her brain in a scramble to come up with someone. She hadn't felt close to anyone for years, not since her illness. Her best friend had moved on, her sister was a stranger to her, her parents were so at war with each other that even after all this time becoming close to either of them was out of the question. Each would see it as betrayal of the other. Those in her current friendship circle knew about her brush with cancer but not about her infertility. No one knew how much her heart ached for what she had lost.

She swallowed tightly and removed his hand from where it was cupping her face, annoyed she hadn't done so as soon as he'd touched her. 'This is highly irregular…you mustn't touch me…like that…not again…'

'Because you like it too much?' His gaze was pointed, his tone mocking.

Emmie raised her chin. 'It would be completely unprofessional of me to encourage your advances.'

He gave an indolent smile that sent another wave of liquid heat to her core. 'Forgive me for misreading the signals.'

Emmie bridled in affront. 'I gave you no signals.' She mentally crossed her fingers over her white lie.

His eyes twinkled knowingly and he gave a mock-bow. 'Come. Let's not quibble over it. I will keep my distance unless you expressly tell me not to.'

'I can assure you that will *never* happen.' Emmie's confident tone didn't quite match how she was feeling on the inside. Matteo Vitale was the most tempting man she had ever met. If he put his mind to seducing her, she wouldn't stand a chance of resisting him.

And she had a horrible feeling he knew it.

Matteo gave Emmie a tour of the estate but stayed well away from the private garden he had made for Abriana and Gabriel. It was in a secluded part of the estate, in an area where his late wife used to spend a lot of time on her own. The reason for that was she had been deeply unhappy, and that had been entirely his fault.

Emmie leaned down to smell one of the old-world roses in the garden closest to the villa. 'Wow, what a heavenly scent.' She straightened and smiled wryly at him. 'I can never decide if roses or sweet peas are my favourite flowers. Or freesias, or lily of the valley… So many to choose from.'

'You can have more than one favourite, surely?'

Her smile faded slightly and her gaze fell away from his. She trailed her fingers across the shell-pink bloom of the full-blown rose in a reflective manner. 'When I was a child, I used to have my own garden where we lived in the country. My parents gave me one plot and my sister the other.' Her hand came back to her side and she let out a long sigh. 'Pot plants aren't quite the same thing, are they?'

'No, not quite.' Matteo walked in step with her along the gravel path, conscious of keeping space between them. He sensed her attraction to him but wondered why she was so adamant not to pursue it. Maintaining a professional distance was advisable, but he had seen the way her gaze kept drifting to his mouth, and had felt the crackling energy that zapped between them from the moment they met. But indulging in a fling with professional match-maker Emmie Woodcroft was not going to achieve his goal of finding a wife. Not unless she herself volunteered for the position. But that was hardly likely—she had already insisted she was a card-carrying member of the single-and-loving-it club.

The question that bugged him was, why? He found it hard to imagine her spending the rest of her life alone. She didn't seem the loner type. Running a professional match-making service seemed an odd choice of career for a loner.

'Is your sister older or younger than you?' Matteo asked in the silence.

'Younger.'

'What does she do for a living?'

Emmie bit her lip and turned to look at the fields in the distance. 'Natalie isn't working at the moment. She's been…unwell for a long time.'

Matteo frowned, wondering if he should press her for more details. He didn't appreciate people prying into his background, but he found he really wanted to know more about Emmie and what had made her the person she was today. She had mentioned during the evening they'd had dinner together that she'd spent some time in hospital as a teenager. Did her sister suffer from the same unspecified illness? 'I'm sorry to hear that.' He figured if she wanted to tell him more, she would do so.

Emmie turned and gave him a stiff smile that wasn't really a smile. 'She has an eating disorder. Anorexia. We've almost lost her several times. It's been such a rollercoaster, trying to keep her from going over the edge.'

Matteo reached for her hand and gently squeezed it in his. 'I'm sorry. That must be terrifying for you and your parents.'

She looked down at their joined hands. He was relieved and secretly delighted she didn't pull away. 'Yes, well, we manage each in our own way…some of us better than others.'

He stroked the back of her hand with his thumb. 'It's a wonder your parents are still together. The stress of an ill child can—'

'They're not.' Emmie's tone was blunt but with a lower note of pain. She slipped her hand out of his and picked another nearby bloom, holding it up to her nose before adding, 'They divorced years ago.'

Matteo was starting to understand Emmie's need to make people happy. She hadn't been able to solve the problems of her sister and parents, so sought to do it for her clients. 'You mentioned when we first met that you'd spent time in and out of hospital. Did you have an eating disorder too?'

She looked at him for a moment before shifting her gaze back to the garden bed. 'No.' She paused for a beat and added, 'I had cancer.'

CHAPTER FIVE

EMMIE CLOSED HER eyes in a tight blink and wished she hadn't spoken. She had known some of her friends for years before she had mentioned the dreaded *C* word. Why, then, had she told Matteo when she had only met him a matter of days ago? Why was her guard slipping when for years it had stayed firmly, resolutely in place? She normally kept a professional distance from her clients. She didn't tell them much about herself because it wasn't about her—it was about her finding them a partner.

But Matteo Vitale was not just a client…he was the first man she had felt attracted to since she'd become ill all those years ago. Really attracted, intensely attracted, to the point where her stoic acceptance of her circumstances was being undermined, like a fine crack in a china tea cup. She had taught herself not to want the things other people wanted, for if she fell in love and then got a recurrence of cancer she would be hurting yet another person. She would have to witness them fall apart just as she had witnessed her mother, father and sister do. Her illness had irreparably hurt everyone she loved. Her mission in life now was to make sure others had the things she could no longer have.

Matteo came closer and laid a gentle hand on the top of her shoulder and turned her to face him. His expression was etched in deep concern. 'Cancer?' His tone was hoarse with shock.

'Lymphoma. Hodgkin's. I was in and out of hospital for two years.' Seriously, she had to learn to keep her mouth shut around him. Next, she'd be telling him all the gory details—how wretchedly ill she'd been with the chemo… how her sense of dignity had completely disappeared the moment she had gone to hospital and had never quite recovered. How guilty she felt about the break-up of her family and her sister's slide into anorexia. How everything had been blown up by the bomb of her cancer.

His hand gently squeezed her shoulder. 'You poor darling, but you're better now, *si*?'

Emmie stretched her lips into a smile. 'But

of course. The chemo worked brilliantly…
Well, eventually, that is.' A little too brilliantly
but, as low as her guard currently was, there
was no way she was going to tell him that little nasty detail.

Matteo's hand fell away from her shoulder
as if he'd only just realised it was still lying
there. 'Cancer is hard enough to face as an
adult but for a child…' He shook his head as
if in disbelief that life could be so cruel. 'It's
unthinkable.'

'I was seventeen, almost an adult.' Emmie
began walking along the garden path again,
keen to avoid his gaze. 'I won't say it wasn't
hard. It was, but it's in the past, and I rarely
think about it now.'

And there was another big fat lie. She *always*
thought about it. Every headache or painful
twinge of a muscle sent her into a mad panic.
Was the lymphoma back? Was she going to die
of some other sort of cancer? Would she have
to go through months and months of torturous
treatment all over again? Would her family and
friends fall apart around her all over again?
The worries were like little gremlins that followed her wherever she went, reminding her
she was on borrowed time and that, one day,
her time might be up sooner rather than later.

* * *

They walked under an archway of the pendulous blooms of fragrant wisteria and Matteo pushed one section aside to let Emmie through. He was still reeling from her revelation about her illness. Cancer was such a frightening diagnosis for anyone to face, much less a teenager. He could only imagine how tough it must have been for her and her family. Facing one's mortality at such a tender age would surely leave an indelible mark on one's character? The more time he spent with Emmie, the more he was intrigued by her character.

'My father refused chemo,' Matteo said after a moment. 'Although, to be fair, the survival rate for lung cancer is abysmally low compared to other cancers, even with chemo or surgery. It's good that you came through with the all-clear. Your parents must have been so relieved.'

'They were but not enough to call off the divorce,' Emmie said with a sigh. 'I sometimes wonder if I hadn't got sick if they'd still be together.'

'Sometimes challenges thrown at a couple shine a light on the cracks that were already there,' Matteo said. 'You shouldn't blame yourself. It wasn't your fault you got cancer. That was sheer bad luck.'

Emmie stopped by the next fragrant garden bed, snapped off a blue love-in-the-mist bloom and twirled the stem between her index finger and thumb. 'I used to grow these in the garden I was telling you about.' She walked a couple more paces and continued, 'We had to sell and move closer to London when I got sick. I cried buckets when we left—not where my parents could see me, of course. But when I was alone.' Her teeth sank into her lower lip and he wondered if she regretted being so open and honest with him.

Matteo was starting to realise there was a lot more to Emmie Woodcroft than he'd first thought. No wonder he found her so intriguing—there were depths and layers to her personality honed out of suffering at such a young age. She had stared down death as a teenager and won, but no doubt there had been a lot of suffering in the process.

And didn't he know a little about suffering from a young age? Not anything as terrifying as cancer, of course, but the walk-out of his mother had been a life-defining moment. A moment he remembered so clearly, *too* clearly. Painfully clearly. If he allowed himself to dwell on it he could still picture her car disappearing into the distance…could still feel the empty ache of despair in his chest…the painful jab of rejection that had never quite gone away but still lay twisted and ugly, deep inside him like a wound, gnarled and ropey with scar tissue.

'Where was your country home?' Matteo asked.

'In Devon. We had a bit of acreage there, not a lot, but it was wonderful not being too close to neighbours.' She gave him a sideways glance and added, 'I'm sorry if I'm boring you.' She gave a self-deprecating laugh, her cheeks going a delicate shade of pink. 'I'm supposed to be getting to know you, not you me. It must be the heady scent of the flowers and the fresh air bewitching me. Tell me to shut up.'

Matteo smiled. 'I like hearing about you.'

She stopped walking to look up at him. 'But I've told you heaps more about myself than you've told me. Tell me something about yourself that no one else knows.'

There were many things Matteo had not told anyone about himself, and he was doing everything in his power to make it stay that way. Not that Emmie Woodcroft made it easy, though. She had a beguiling nature that had a potent effect on his resolve. But he considered his back story irrelevant to the task at hand. He needed her to find him a suitable wife and the sooner she got on with it, the better. Playing twenty questions was not his thing at all.

He glanced at his watch in a pointed manner. 'We'll have to save this conversation for another time. Can you find your way back to the villa from here? I have to see one of my staff about something before dinner.'

'Sure, but I'm going to ask you again over dinner, so don't think you're getting off so easily.'

Matteo forced a smile. 'You're a determined little thing, aren't you?'

Her eyes twinkled like the sunlight dancing on the water-lily pond behind her. 'It's how I succeed at my job. And you do want me to succeed, don't you?'

'But of course.' Matteo was paying her a small fortune to do as he requested. It was a pity her methods included digging for emotions he had long ago buried.

But he was going to damn well keep them that way.

Emmie was enjoying the early-evening summer sunshine too much to go back to the villa straight away. The air was fragrant with flowers and the scent of freshly mown grass and the light breeze had taken the harsh sting out of the sun's heat. She wandered along the crushed limestone path, past the water feature, stopping every now and again to smell yet another heady bloom of the exquisite roses. Blooms as big as saucers, petals as soft as velvet, the mix of fragrances so intense it was intoxicating to her senses.

Or maybe that had more to do with being with Matteo Vitale…

Emmie knew she had to stop thinking about him in that way—the way that would only lead to disappointment, if not heartbreak. She might sense his attraction to her, and she was in no doubt of her attraction to him, but it couldn't go anywhere. How could it? She couldn't provide him with the thing he most needed—an heir. But she could hopefully provide him with a wife from her list of clients, for that was what he was paying her to do.

The kicker was, what woman in her right mind would marry him when he had no intention of falling in love with her? Love was what her clients were seeking, not a marriage of convenience, even if it was to one of the most handsome and wealthiest men Emmie had ever encountered. Of course, it was true that occasionally marriages of conveniences worked out well for some couples, mutual love developing over time, and the relationship strengthening and growing into one of joy and long-term happiness.

Some distance from the path, Emmie noticed a small rivulet that fed into the river running through the estate. A family of wood ducks waddled near the banks and, dying for a better glimpse of the cute little fluffy ducklings, Emmie walked towards it through a wilder section of the garden.

The family of ducks had by now slipped into the water and was swimming away, but then Emmie noticed a chest-high hedge in the distance close to a thickly wooded area. The hedge enclosed a squared-off area that appeared to be some sort of private garden with a large shady tree in the centre. She had to step across the rivulet to get to it, which was not all that easy to do. There was no bridge, and the stones that were there were slippery with moss, but somehow, she managed it without falling in. When she got closer, she found a rustic wrought-iron gate set in the hedge. She turned the handle and pushed the gate open and stepped into the cool shady enclosure.

And then she saw the white head stones over two graves.

The leaves rustled above her head like the breath of a ghost and a shiver tiptoed over Emmie's scalp, and then all the way down her spine. There was an adult grave and a smaller one…so small it could only be that of a child. Her heart gave a painful spasm… A very small child—a baby. A tiny baby. There were fresh flowers in the brass vases and a teddy bear encased in a glass box on the baby's grave.

Emmie moved closer to the head stones and knelt on the soft grass to read the inscriptions.

Abriana Maria Vitale,
wife of Matteo Andrea Vitale,
loving mother of Gabriel Giorgio Vitale

The rest of the words were in Italian, but Emmie could see from the dates that Abriana had died eight years ago at the age of twenty-five. And the baby…she swallowed a thick lump in her throat…the baby had died on the day it was born, presumably at the same time as his mother.

Emmie sat back on her heels in shock, her heart contracting as though it was in a vice. Her fingers and toes went numb as if the blood had left her extremities to pump to her vital organs. Matteo had been married? He'd tragically lost his wife and baby and yet hadn't told her? Why not? It was the most important information about him and yet he had kept it from her.

A cold shiver coursed down her spine and her stomach churned with anguish. Such a terrible, heart-wrenching tragedy to go through and yet it explained so much about his personality. The harsh landscape of his face, his perpetual frown, the lines of pain etched into his skin, the shadows in his eyes, his set mouth that so rarely smiled, as if he had forgotten how to… No wonder he was furious about his father's will—Matteo was still grieving the loss of his young wife and child. No wonder he baulked at the idea of marrying. He wasn't ready to move on with his life but the will left him no choice.

But why were his wife and child buried here and not at the local cemetery Emmie had driven past on her way to the estate? There were no other graves, so this was not a family plot with the rest of Matteo's ancestors. His father had died recently and there was no sign of his grave here. Just these two lonely graves hidden in a secluded green area of the estate.

There was the snap of a twig behind Emmie and she jumped in alarm and scrambled to her feet to see Matteo only a few feet away, his expression hard to read, given the angle of light, for his face was entirely in shadow.

'So, you've found them.' His tone gave her no clue as to how he felt about her stumbling across his wife and child's graves. It was flat, toneless, empty.

Emmie brushed her breeze-teased hair back off her face. 'Matteo... I don't understand. Why didn't you tell me you were married and had a child?'

He moved closer to the graves and stood looking down at them with his hands shoved into the pockets of his chinos. 'I don't like talking about that period of my life.'

'I can only imagine how terribly painful it must be, but surely you see—'

'You can't possibly understand,' he said, turning to look at her with a savage frown. 'So don't insult me by pretending you do.'

'I understand grief is a very personal thing,' Emmie said. 'That it's painful, and a process that can takes years if not a lifetime to work through. Losing someone you love is one of the most devastating things that can—'

'But that's the point.' Matteo's voice hardened. 'I didn't love Abriana, not the way she deserved to be loved. Not the way she wanted to be loved.'

Emmie looked at him in shock, her mind whirling. Then why had he married her? She glanced back at the tiny grave next to his wife's and bit her lip, joining the dots herself. 'It was because of the baby? Your marriage, I mean? Because of Gabriel?'

He flinched as if the very sound of that tiny baby's name was an arrow to his heart. 'We had dated on and off for a month or two. She told me she was on the pill and, even though we always used condoms, she somehow got pregnant.' He scraped a hand through his hair. 'I understood and respected her wish to keep the baby. But I wanted my child to grow up with my name, so I offered to marry her.'

'But neither of you were happy.' Emmie didn't state it as a question for she could see there was no point. The answer was in the ravaged lines of Matteo's face, a road map of pain and grief and guilt.

'No, not for one moment.' He turned back to look at the graves of his wife and child, his shoulders hunched forward, tension visible in the muscles of his back and shoulders.

Emmie came up beside him and placed a gentle hand on the small of his back. He gave a light shudder, like a stallion shivering a fly off its hide. 'I'm so very sorry…' she whispered.

There was a long silence broken only by the tinkling of water nearby and the gentle rustling of the leaves above of the large tree casting its sheltering shade.

Matteo took a ragged breath and stepped back from the graves. 'Abriana was a nice person. A decent person. She would have been a wonderful mother, but even that was taken away from her. She never even got to hold our child in her arms.'

'What happened?'

'A car crash. She was driving back from a pre-natal appointment and a car crossed into her path on a narrow bend. She made it to hospital but died a short time later. They delivered Gabriel but he…' He swallowed and continued in a hollow voice, 'He only lived for two hours. I didn't get back from London until later that evening.'

Emmie blinked back the sting of tears and touched him on the arm. 'Oh, Matteo, how tragic. How terribly sad and tragic.'

Matteo covered her hand with his and gave it a squeeze, his expression still grim. 'I swore I would never marry again. I don't consider myself cut out for marriage and all it entails. If I had been a better husband, then maybe Abriana would still be here, and Gabriel too.' He removed his hand from hers and thrust it back in his trouser pocket. 'But of course, my father had other ideas, and decided to force my hand.'

Emmie frowned. 'So, that's why he wrote the codicil on his will? To force you to marry again and produce an heir?'

'Thoughtful of him, *si*?' His sarcasm wasn't wasted on her. She knew all about manipulative fathers. Her father had played a few manipulative games in his time and caused no end of stress in order to get his own way. But what if Matteo's father had acted out of concern for Matteo? Wanting him to move on with his life instead of being stuck in a deep well of grief and regret? Perhaps his actions were motivated out of love and concern, not a desire to cause further pain.

'You know, there could be another way of looking at your father's motives,' Emmie said. 'He might have wanted you to forgive yourself for what happened with Abriana and Gabriel and to move on with your life.'

'Forgive myself?' Matteo's frown was so deep it carved a deep trench between the dark flashing orbs of his eyes. 'And how am I supposed to do that with them both lying there in the ground?' He waved his hand at the graves. 'I blame myself for everything. How can I not?'

Emmie rolled her lips together, her heart aching for the pain she could sense in every fibre of his being. 'You told me it wasn't my fault I got cancer. It's not your fault your wife and baby died. You weren't driving the car and, besides, you said the other driver crossed to the wrong side of the road. It was their fault, if anyone's.'

'But I *should* have been driving that day,' Matteo said through tightly set lips. 'Abriana wanted me to attend that appointment with her but I chose to go to London instead. I had a court case I was working on for a client, but I could have waited one more day before flying back to London.' He muttered a curse and added with a bitter edge to his voice, 'So don't tell me it's not my fault.' He swung away, walked back through the gate in the hedge and disappeared from sight.

Emmie let out a long sigh but didn't follow him through the gate. She needed time to process what he had told her, to get her head around the tragedy that had shaped him into the man he was today. He was tortured by the grief and guilt of his wife's and baby's deaths, which was completely understandable. Some people never got over such a loss and carried it with them for the rest of their lives.

It seemed more and more obvious to her that Matteo Vitale's father had changed his will to force his son to marry again and produce an heir to continue the family line, knowing that without such an impetus Matteo would be stuck in a prison of self-blame for ever. And, while Matteo was reluctant, he was prepared to fulfil the terms of his father's will—some would say in rather a ruthless manner—in order to save the estate. The estate where his wife and child were buried in this sad little garden.

No wonder Matteo was so keen to keep the estate in his possession. The stakes were higher than Emmie had realised, and it all made sense now. How he had insisted she act with haste in finding him a suitable partner. She had thought him ruthless and a little unfeeling when he'd come into her office that first day, but now she understood his motivation and couldn't help feeling sorry for the horrible dilemma he faced. She wished he had told her from the get-go, but a part of her understood why he hadn't. He was a loner, a deeply private person who would not go public with his pain.

She was reminded again of the wounded wolf image—the alpha male taking himself away from the pack to lick his wounds in private, unwilling to show any hint of vulnerability. There was an element of that same behaviour in her own personality, an unwillingness to share with anyone the deepest agonies of her soul.

But, if Matteo married again without love being part of the equation, it would make it yet another marriage of convenience. Surely that wasn't wise? Such a marriage had already ended in tragedy. Emmie believed in the power of love and, while she had ruled it out for herself, she knew Matteo was someone who was worthy of being loved, if only he would allow himself to love in return. To open his guarded heart and allow it to feel the love she was sure he was more than capable of feeling. But the desertion of his mother when he'd been a young child had made him wary of engaging his emotions.

From the moment she'd met him, Matteo had given her the impression his heart was bricked up behind a thick wall of cynicism. He had told her he had never been in love and she suspected he would never allow himself to be. Matteo had experienced untold pain and loss and had come to her out of desperation to solve his problem. He was paying her a lot of money to find him a wife, to match him with someone who would provide him with an heir.

Emmie released another sigh and turned to look at the head stones standing side by side with only the sound of the birds and the breeze keeping them company in the cool, green shade. The clock was ticking. She had to find him a wife, otherwise he would lose everything, including this sacred ground where his wife and child were buried.

CHAPTER SIX

MATTEO WAS FURIOUS with himself for not realising Emmie might discover Abriana's and Gabriel's graves when he'd left her to make her way back to the villa. Her inquisitive nature, especially in finding out everything she could about him, should have been warning enough but he had ignored it.

But, strangely, there was a part of him that had wanted her to discover the secret pain of his past. Not that he felt any better for revealing it to her. If anything, he felt worse. Emmie would no doubt want to talk more about the tragedy and it would bring it all back—the harrowing guilt. It was a gnawing pain inside him, a constant reminder of how he had failed to keep safe those under his care and protection.

And now, his late father had demanded he commit to another marriage and risk the same happening all over again. But he couldn't walk away from the estate and see it pass into a stranger's hands. He had to do everything in his power to keep it in his possession—it was the price he must pay for having failed to keep his wife and child safe. He owed it to them to honour their memory.

Could Emmie be the answer? The thought was growing deeper roots in his brain. She claimed she wasn't looking for love. That her focus was her business, not finding happiness for herself. A marriage of convenience between them could work if he could convince her to agree to it. Their mutual attraction was undeniable and increasingly irresistible. But he would have to be patient in talking her round. He didn't want to pressure her but surely, she could sense the connection that had developed between them? He wondered if that was why she had been trying to keep her distance since they'd kissed at her house in London. Unless he was misreading the signals, the temptation to explore the chemistry between them was as tempting to her as it was to him.

And he was determined to act on it.

Valentina informed Emmie through a combination of sign language and broken English that dinner would be served in the smaller of the two dining rooms on the ground floor, overlooking the lake. Emmie changed into a dress and scooped up her hair up into a make-shift bun and applied some light make-up. On her way downstairs, she stopped to look at some of the art work, some of which included portraits of Matteo's ancestors. She could see the likeness, particularly in what appeared to be his grandfather Giorgio's portrait. She recalled Matteo's baby son's full name, and that Giorgio had been included in it. Did that mean Matteo had had a special connection with his grandfather? One he hadn't had with his father?

Emmie walked further along the gallery with an even deeper understanding of Matteo's reluctance to lose the estate, notwithstanding it being the final resting place of his wife and child. This was the home of his ancestors, the place where they had lived and loved for hundreds of years. She had found it devastating to move from her childhood home and she had only lived there for seventeen years. How much worse to lose the home that contained so many centuries of history, so many memories?

Emmie came to a door at the end of the gallery that was slightly ajar and her curiosity soon got the better of her. She gently pushed it open and stepped inside to find a library with floor-to-ceiling bookshelves, a mezzanine level and a wooden ladder for access to the higher shelves. There was a beautiful antique desk in polished walnut set in front of tall windows draped with heavy velvet curtains in a deep red the same colour as one of the roses she had smelled that afternoon.

Emmie moved closer to the desk and ran her fingers along the polished surface. She sat on the studded leather chair and swung it from side to side, wondering why Matteo had no photos or sentimental artefacts on his desk as so many people did. There was only a laptop and a blank notepad and a collection of pens and a glass paperweight.

'Looking for more of my secrets?' Matteo's deep voice at the door startled her into standing upright, her cheeks instantly flooding with heat.

'I'm sorry. I was just having a look around. It's a beautiful room…so many books. Some of them must be so old. Have you had them valued? There might be first editions in that collection and they're worth a fortune.' Emmie knew she was rambling, desperate to fill the silence, desperate to avoid the censure and cynicism of his gaze.

'Yes, well, it will be a pain to have to move them if I am unable to fulfil the terms of my father's will in time.' He glanced around the room before bringing his gaze back to hers. 'But, all being well, it won't come to that.'

Emmie moved out from behind the desk. 'Your situation is…complicated. I can see that now. I understand your reluctance to marry again but this time around might work out brilliantly. Lots of cultures rely on arranged marriages and using a dating agency is a little like that. Matching people who are most likely to fall in love.'

'I'm not interested in falling in love. All I'm interested in is fulfilling the terms of my father's will.'

'But surely you could do both?' Emmie said. 'You shouldn't rule it out. Love can strike when you least expect it.'

Matteo came to where she was standing and her senses reeled at the force of energy he brought with him. Sensual energy, a dark, brooding energy, that sent livewires of awareness flickering across her skin. She had to hyper-extend her neck to keep eye contact and her stomach swooped at the deep blue of his glinting eyes.

'And has love ever struck you?' His voice

was low and deep, and caused a riot of sensations to flutter in her core.

Emmie disguised a swallow, her pulse hammering, her heart racing. 'No. I haven't been in love before...'

A cynical light gleamed in his gaze. 'And why is that, do you think?' He ran an idle finger down the curve of her cheek, setting spot fires in her flesh.

'I—I'm too busy finding love for my clients...' Emmie was annoyed her voice was so whispery and her heart rate so erratic and her resolve to resist him so absent. She was acting like a love-struck schoolgirl in front of a much-adored celebrity. The sheer magnetism of him overwhelmed her, bewitching her into a mesmerised trance. She couldn't drag her gaze away from his mouth, the sculptured perfection of it, the firm lines of his top lip and the fullness of his lower lip that hinted at a potent, bone-melting sensuality.

Matteo sent the pad of his thumb across her bottom lip in a spine-tingling stroke. 'You have such a beautiful mouth...' His voice had lowered another semitone. 'I keep thinking about how it felt to kiss you that evening at your house.'

Emmie wasn't aware of moving but suddenly she was pressed against him, chest to chest, thigh to thigh, her gaze locked on his, her heart threatening to punch its way out of her body. 'Matteo…' She could barely get her voice to work, barely think straight—all she wanted was to feel his mouth press down on hers. It was a burning need inside her, a fervent need that would not be tamed any other way. 'Kiss me.' She could hardly believe she had spoken her need out loud, even if it had only been a whisper—a desperate whisper.

The smouldering heat in his gaze intensified, as if the fire he had stirred in her flesh had travelled to his. His thumb passed over her lower lip once more, slowly, torturously slowly, making her flesh tingle with increasing want. A want so agonisingly intense it consumed her, controlled her, overpowered her.

'I've had a burning desire to do so almost from the first moment I met you and every moment since.' His warm breath mingled with hers in the intimate space between their mouths.

Emmie stood on tiptoe and laced her hands around his neck, worried he might change his mind and pull away. Her breasts were crushed against the hard wall of his chest, her thighs pressed into the firmness of his, her senses doing cartwheels as she felt the stirring of his erection against her body. Desire rippled through her in a torrent, a flash flood of fiery heat that left no part of her unaffected. Her inner core pulsed with longing, a deep, throbbing pulse that turned her to molten liquid. 'Then do it. Do it now. Kiss me. I want you to.' She didn't care that she was close to begging—all she cared about was feeling his sensual mouth pressed to hers again, feeling the desire he felt for her against her lips.

He gave a low groan deep in his throat and then his mouth came down on hers, his lips firm, urgent, masterful, demanding. Emmie responded with the same urgency, hungry for the exquisite taste of him, the incendiary heat and fire of his mouth sending shock waves through her body. Delicious, shuddering shock waves that awakened every nerve in her flesh.

Emmie murmured her approval against his lips. His tongue stroked the seam of her mouth in a spine-loosening movement and she welcomed him in with a whimper of pleasure. His tongue touched hers and an explosion of sensations shot through her, sending waves of heat to her core. He deepened the kiss, stirring her into a fervent response that was so erotic, so electric, so exciting, it set her pulse madly racing.

One of his hands came up to cup her face and the other went to the small of her back, bringing her body closer to the hot, hard heat of his growing erection. Emmie whimpered again in excitement, relishing the feel of his aroused flesh against her. Nothing could have prepared her for the magic of his explosive kiss, the potent power of his lips and tongue making every cell of her body shout in rapturous joy.

Matteo angled his head to shift position and another guttural groan came from his throat, his lips firmer, more demanding, signalling an escalating need so similar to the one pounding through her flesh. One of his hands went to the back of her head, his fingers clutching a handful of her hair, not roughly, but not gently either, just somewhere delightfully, thrillingly, in between. Ripples of pleasure ran down her spine, her inner core throbbing with the need for his erotic, intimate possession.

'Are you okay with me doing this?' He spoke just above her mouth, the movement of his breath like a caress on her sensitised lips.

'More than okay,' Emmie said against his lips. 'It's just a kiss, right?' She wanted more, much more, but didn't know if it was wise to take things that far. She had for so long ignored her body's needs. They hummed occasionally, in the background, but she had taught herself to ignore them. But now, in Matteo Vitale's arms, she caught a tempting glimpse of what making love with him would be like—thrilling, mind-blowing, earth-shattering.

If she succumbed to the temptation, nothing would be the same again. *She* would not be the same.

Matteo framed her face with his hands, his gaze searching. 'Is it?'

Emmie stroked her hand down the length of his lean jaw, her soft skin catching on his light stubble, sending another wave of shivering sensations down her spine. 'You're a very attractive man, and I'm only human, but anything more than a kiss or two is probably not wise under the circumstances.' She removed her hand from his face but he captured it and held it against his chest instead, his eyes smouldering.

'Because?' he prompted.

Emmie moistened her lips with the point of her tongue, her stomach swooping when his gaze followed the movement. 'I need to maintain a professional distance in order to do what you're paying me to do.' She tugged her hand out from underneath his and stepped back. 'I came here to find out everything I can about you so I can match you with the perfect partner.'

'Allowing me to kiss you is part of your research, *si*?' There was a sardonic light in his deep-blue eyes.

'No, it is not.' Emmie could feel her cheeks heating and turned away to regain her composure. She picked up the paperweight from his desk and tested its weight in her hand. 'Why don't you have any photos of your wife in the villa?' She put the paperweight down and turned and faced him. 'I've looked in most of the rooms and there's nothing. Only portraits of your ancestors.'

'We didn't have that sort of relationship.' He moved across the room to straighten a couple of books on the bookshelves, his back turned towards her.

'Describe your relationship with her.'

Matteo turned to face her, his expression grim. 'It wasn't intimate.'

'Did you share a room? A bed?'

'No.'

Emmie frowned. 'Why not? You were husband and wife.'

He gave a movement of his lips that was one-part smile, three-parts grimace. 'I didn't think it was wise or indeed fair to encourage her feelings for me.'

Something tightened around Emmie's heart—a painful tug of invisible stitches. 'She was in love with you?'

A shadow moved through his gaze and his jaw tightened. 'So she said, but I could not return her feelings. I liked her, cared about her, but as to love, that sort of love...' He gave a one-shouldered shrug. 'It's not an emotion I've felt for her or for anyone.'

'Would you recognise it if you did?'

A cynical smile slanted his mouth. 'Romantics such as yourself would say so, would they not?'

'But what do *you* think?'

Matteo came back over to her and lifted her chin with the end of his index finger, locking his gaze with hers. 'I think you ask a lot of questions that you would not answer yourself.'

Emmie's heart began to thump, her breath stalling in her throat. 'I think I would recognise it if I fell in love with someone.' Her voice came out scratchy.

His hand cupped one side of her face, his eyes still unwavering on hers. 'What do you think you would feel? Describe it for me.'

Emmie sent her tongue across her lips

again, her pulse racing so fast she felt light-headed… Or maybe that was because she was mesmerised by the deep, rumbling tone of his voice, the warm cradle of his hand against her face, the proximity of his tempting body and her own body's craving, driving need for more of his touch. Never had she been so aware of a man. Aware of every nuance of his expression, every soft, warm waft of his breath against her mouth.

'Having never been in love, I can only go on what other people have said. That you just know with a certainty that this person is the only one for you. You know it like it was written in stone. That it was meant to be from before you were even born. That this person is the one who completes you, complements and fulfils you in a way no one else can do.'

His gaze was unwavering. 'So, you believe there is only one perfect partner for each person?'

Emmie eased out of his hold and made a point of putting some distance between them. 'What I tell my clients to concentrate on is being a perfect partner themselves rather than expecting to find someone who is perfect for them. Working on yourself first is key. Too many relationships fail when one partner shines a light on the other's imperfections without examining and working on their own.'

Matteo gave a rueful movement of his lips. 'Wise words.' He picked up a pen from his desk and stroked his fingers along its slim barrel, his forehead creased in a frown.

Emmie studied him for a long moment, wondering if he was thinking about his late wife. 'Were you overly critical of Abriana?'

He put the pen down and met her gaze head on. 'Not at all.'

'But she was critical of you.' Emmie didn't phrase it as a question.

'And why shouldn't she have been? She wanted me to fall in love with her the way she had fallen in love with me.' His lips twisted into another grimace. 'It's not a comfortable feeling, knowing you've broken someone's heart.'

'But you were honest with her from the get-go? I mean, you didn't say things you didn't mean to get her to marry you once you knew she was pregnant?'

'I was brutally honest.'

Emmie could well believe it. 'And you were absolutely certain Gabriel was your child?'

'Absolutely.'

'You asked for a paternity test?'

'No.'

Emmie raised her brows. 'Why not? How well did you know her? She might have been—'

'I didn't ask, but she insisted on having one done so there was no question over paternity.'

'I guess, given your forensically trained mind, she felt she had to.'

'Perhaps.'

There was a silence that was so thick Emmie could almost hear the tiny dust motes moving through the air.

Matteo moved to the door, his expression inscrutable. 'Come. Valentina will be waiting for us with our dinner.'

Emmie followed him out of the library, conscious of him walking by her side down the long, wide corridor…conscious of the brush of his arm against hers…conscious of the taste of him still lingering in her mouth. And conscious of the needs he had awakened that still hummed in her flesh.

CHAPTER SEVEN

DINNER WAS A beautiful meal prepared with fresh produce from the estate, and Emmie delighted in every dish that was brought to the table. Valentina's cooking took the whole pasture-to-plate trend to a whole new level. Succulent asparagus in a creamy hollandaise, trout caught from the river and pan-fried, served with an Italian-style salsa, and to follow a delectable honey-flavoured panna cotta garnished with plump strawberries.

'Your housekeeper could open her own restaurant,' Emmie said, finally putting down her cutlery with a sigh of pleasure. 'Seriously, that was one of the best meals I've eaten in ages.'

'Don't tempt her to leave me,' Matteo said with a wry smile, pouring a fresh serving of mineral water into Emmie's glass.

Emmie leaned her head on one side to study

him. 'So, you can form deep attachments to people, then?'

He made a harrumphing sound. 'Valentina and I go a long way back, even before she came to work for me.'

'She's old enough to be your mother,' Emmie mused.

'Precisely.'

'So, she's kind of a maternal figure to you?'

'*Si*, and one I deeply admire. She was unable to have children of her own and her husband left her because if it.' He picked up his glass of ruby-red wine but didn't raise it to his lips. 'She never got over it. She hasn't had another relationship and instead has devoted her life to working for me.' He took a token sip of his wine and put the glass back on the table.

Emmie wondered if Valentina's infertility was the most heart-breaking thing for her or the rejection of her husband. Was that why she had never married again? 'That's sad… I mean, that she hasn't had the family she longed for. She must have been devastated when you lost your wife and baby.'

Something flickered across his face. '*Si*, she was, but unfortunately she and Abriana did not get on well.' His lips moved in a grim twist.

'Valentina didn't think Abriana was the right partner for me.'

'Because you weren't in love with her?'

'That and other reasons.'

'Such as?'

Matteo gave his mouth another twist. 'I don't wish to speak ill of the dead. Abriana did her best under difficult circumstances.'

Emmie secretly admired him for not spilling all about his late wife's shortcomings. Too many of her clients spoke at length about how awful their previous partners were and it always rang alarm bells for her. The talking down of a previous partner often showed her far more things about the client than their ex. But Matteo had clearly respected Abriana even if he hadn't loved her the way she had wanted him to. 'Can I ask you something?'

'Go ahead.' His tone was bland but his gaze was watchful. Guarded.

'Why didn't you bury Abriana and Gabriel at the cemetery in the village? Why here, on the estate? And in that particular spot?'

Matteo's expression clouded and she got a glimpse of the pain he was so good at hiding most of the time. 'Abriana loved that shady area away from the villa. She used to go down there with a book and read for hours.'

His broad shoulders slumped, as if weighted down by the burden of sad memories and painful regrets. 'I didn't think she would want to spend eternity in a cold impersonal graveyard amongst strangers, but rather somewhere she felt at peace.'

His actions showed a deeper sensitivity than Emmie had given him credit for. 'It's a beautiful spot...so tranquil and serene.' She picked up her water glass for something to do with her hands. 'Do you go there often?'

Another shadow passed through his gaze. 'Every day when I am home.' Another rueful twist of his mouth. 'Abriana would find it amusing that I have spent far more time down there now than I did with her when she was alive.' His attempt at wry humour fell a little short of the mark and it showed in his tone and on his features.

Emmie put her glass back down and reached for his forearm where it rested on the table. She gave his firm flesh a gentle press. 'I'm sure she would appreciate the respect you pay her and Gabriel.' Her own voice betrayed her see-sawing emotions. She was not normally a teary person—facing down death at a young age had taught her that tears couldn't change difficult circumstances. But Matteo's situation was so tragic, and the self-recrimination he flayed himself with was painful to witness. Her heart ached for Abriana who had died so young, and for little Gabriel, who had never felt the shelter of his mother's arms in the two-hour span of his tiny life.

Matteo placed his hand on top of hers. *'Grazie.'* His voice was deep and husky, his eyes dark and tortured.

Emmie bit down on her lower lip, trying to contain her feelings, but the sting of tears at the back of her eyes made her vision blur. 'Did you get to…to hold him? To hold your son before he…?' She found she couldn't say the word, that dreadfully final word—*died.*

Matteo's dark gaze shone with moisture and her heart twisted again. *'Si,* I held him.' His throat moved up and down over a tight swallow. 'But not while he was alive. I got there too late. It is my biggest regret, and I cannot escape it, no matter how much I try.' He suddenly scraped back his chair and stood. 'Will you excuse me? Valentina will show you to your room. It's been a long day and I'm sure you're ready for bed. Goodnight.' A shutter had come down over his features like a curtain on a stage, his tone polite but formal, distant and unreachable.

'Goodnight…' Emmie could barely get her voice above a mumble and, right at that moment, she didn't trust her legs to get her out of the chair. She sat in silence for endless minutes, staring sightlessly at the remains of their meal and the flickering candle on the table, wondering if Matteo would ever come to a point when he would forgive himself and finally move on with his life. Or would he be chained to the past with shackles of regret and self-blame for ever?

Matteo strode out of the villa and into the moonlit garden, desperate for air, desperate to escape the pain of his failure to protect his own flesh and blood. It was a gut-wrenching pain that tortured him daily and never more so than when he was home on the estate. Every time he visited the graves of his wife and son, he revisited his failure. To think their lives had been cut short because he hadn't been there when they'd needed him was an inescapable reality. He should have been driving Abriana to that appointment. She hadn't been a confident driver and she had spoken to him about having 'baby brain,' when she lost concentration at times. How could he forgive himself for not doing all he could to keep she and the baby safe?

He was shocked at how much he had revealed to Emmie in the short time he had known her. She had a way of getting under his guard with her active listening and gentle questioning, making him *want* to tell her more. Making him want to relieve himself of the burden of carrying this load of guilt that never seemed to lessen even though eight years had passed. But Emmie Woodcroft was not a grief counsellor, she was a professional matchmaker, and he needed her to do her thing so he could keep the estate secure.

But his attraction to her was proving harder and harder to resist. Emmie had asked him to kiss her and he had done so with such ardour it had shaken him to the core. She stirred in him a ferocious lust that stormed through his body like a red-hot fever. Her mouth was sweet, yet dangerously tempting. Everything about her was dangerously tempting. But his ardour was more than matched by hers for him. It had been electrifying to hold her in his arms, to explore her soft and yielding mouth with his own. His body still hummed with the need she had awakened. It was distracting to have her here, to say the least, especially when she was supposed to be finding him a wife.

A wayward thought drifted into his mind... *You could have a fling with her in order to convince her to marry you.*

The more he thought about it, the more attractive the prospect became—and all the more deliciously tempting. There was a definite spark between them, a hot, bright spark he hadn't felt quite as intensely with anyone else. Emmie Woodcroft, with her luscious mouth and spine-tingling touch, made him hard as stone and aching with forbidden longing. But perhaps, after offering her a short fling, Emmie might be more open to the idea of marrying him, thus helping him fulfil the terms of his father's will.

For, if he didn't marry soon and gain an heir, he would lose the estate for ever. And that didn't bear thinking about.

Emmie was sure she would never be able to get to sleep that night but she drifted off more or less as soon as her head landed on the satin-covered pillow. But some time during the wee hours she heard a sound that had her sitting bolt-upright in her bed. She shivered even though the room wasn't cold. The moon shone in from the windows, and she strained her ears to listen out for a repeat of the sound.

The night was silent for so long, she thought she must have dreamt the sound or maybe even uttered it herself. But then, just as she was about to settle back down, she heard it again—a low, deep howl of pain that tore at her heartstrings. She pushed back the covers and grabbed her wrap and hastily put it on over her nightgown, tied the waist ties and padded out to the corridor. The sound had come from Matteo's suite a little further down the long, wide corridor, and before she could stop and think about what she was doing, or why she was even doing it, she went towards his closed door and gave it a soft rap with her knuckles.

'Matteo?'

There was no sound other than the rustling of bed linen, as if he was thrashing about. Emmie turned the handle and pushed the door open a fraction, the moonlight shining a wide, silver beam across Matteo's rumpled bed, where he was lying in a state of agitation, although he was obviously still asleep. Emmie had had nightmares for years after her cancer scare, so recognised the signs immediately.

She padded over to the bed and gently

stroked him on the shoulder. 'Matteo. Wake up. You're having a bad dream.'

He suddenly sat up and one of his strong hands flashed out and gripped her by the wrist. His hold was almost cruelly tight and a flicker of fear whipped through her. His hair was tousled, his upper body naked, the lower part covered by the sheet. *Was he completely naked under that sheet?* The thought sent a delicious thrill through her body. The ripped and coiled muscles of his abdomen made her fingers itch to caress them, to see if they were as hard as they looked.

Matteo blinked as if to clear his vision but his hold was still painfully tight around her wrist. 'What are you doing in my bedroom?' His voice was a low growl, his eyes dark and brooding, the generous peppering of ink-black stubble around his jaw making him look menacing, almost dangerous.

Emmie tried to ignore the leap of her pulse, the hot spurt of longing that smouldered in her core and the crackling of dark sexual energy that sparked in the air. 'I heard you call out... I—I was worried about you.' She tugged at his hold, wincing slightly. 'Could you relax your grip a bit?'

A flicker of shock passed over his features

and his fingers fell away from her wrist. 'I'm sorry.' His voice was hoarse, his expression tortured with self-loathing. 'Did I hurt you?' He snapped on the bedside lamp and Emmie quickly covered the noticeably red marks on her wrist with her other hand.

'No. Not at all. I'm fine, really.'

'Let me see.' His voice brooked no resistance and she meekly raised her wrist for his inspection. He swallowed deeply and ever so gently cradled her wrist in his hand, as if it were a fragile piece of blown glass. One of his fingers traced over each of the red marks, and then he lifted her wrist to his mouth and pressed a barely touching kiss to her skin. She shivered as his lips caressed each mark, her heart beginning to thrum with excitement, her lower body stirring with feminine longing.

Matteo's eyes met hers and the atmosphere tightened with an almost audible click. He released her wrist to stroke his hand down the curve of her cheek. 'You shouldn't have come in here.' His voice contained a note of reprimand that somehow made her flesh tingle all over again.

'Why?'

His eyes drifted to her mouth. 'I think you know why.'

Emmie stroked her hand down his face, her soft skin catching on his stubble, making another frisson of delight course through her body. 'What do you think might happen?' She was a little shocked at how flirty she sounded, so recklessly flirty.

His eyes moved between hers in a back and forth fashion, every now and again flicking to her mouth as if drawn there by an irresistible force. The same irresistible force that was drawing her gaze to his mouth, aching for him to press it to her own. 'You might regret this in the morning.' His voice was still pitched low and deep, so deep it sounded like the rumble of distant thunder.

Emmie trailed her index finger across his top lip, slowly outlining the firm contour before moving to his fuller lower lip. 'What is there to regret between two consenting adults who desire each other?'

One side of his mouth tilted, his eyes glinting. He placed his hands on her hips, drawing her closer to him on the bed. 'Nothing, if both adults agree on the terms.'

Emmie licked her lips, her heart going like a hyper-active jackhammer in her chest. The smell of him was intoxicating, the press of his hands on her hips sending her senses into a tailspin, the thought of being intimate with him driving her wild with desire. 'The no-strings thing?' She injected her tone with playfulness, keen to show him she wanted nothing more than this stolen moment in time. Their relationship couldn't go anywhere. How could it? She couldn't give him what he most wanted and needed. 'I'm okay with that.'

Matteo pressed the thick pad of his thumb against her lower lip, then he moved it back and forth in a slow caress that sent buzzing sensations through her flesh. The wizardry of his touch was mesmerising. She had no thought of resisting him, no thought of putting a stop to this madness—all she could do was relish the throbbing energy that vibrated between them. 'I can't afford to be distracted right now,' he said but she got the feeling he was saying it for his own benefit rather than hers.

'I know, so why don't we just enjoy the moment?' Since when had she been a living-in-the-moment girl? Never. But this felt right. It felt necessary. It felt important enough to put all other counter arguments to one side. Emmie *wanted* him. Wanted to be wanted by him. Wanted to experience a stolen moment in his arms so she could feed off the memories later. She hadn't been touched by a man other than a doctor or nurse since she'd been diagnosed all those years ago. Why shouldn't she indulge in this moment of madness? This passion had unexpectedly flared between them and she desperately wanted to explore it, even though it was completely out of character for her to do so, especially with a client.

But Matteo Vitale was not just a client—he was the first man who had made her feel powerful as a woman. He awakened in her a sensuality she hadn't known she possessed.

His frown deepened a fraction. 'What happens in Umbria stays in Umbria. Is that what you're saying?'

Emmie moved her mouth closer to his, so close she could feel the warm waft of his breath against her lips. 'That's exactly what I'm saying.'

Matteo made a rough sound in his throat and closed the distance between their mouths in a drugging kiss that made her gasp in delight. His lips moved with urgency against hers, his tongue demanding entry, and she opened to him with another whimper of pleasure. Their tongues met like two hot flames from separate fires, causing a combustion of sensual energy that flared throughout her body in molten heat. His taste was both familiar yet exotically strange—a taste she was rapidly developing a hunger for like an addict does a forbidden drug. It sent her blood racing through her veins at breakneck speed, making every inch of her skin tingle with the need to feel his hands gliding over it.

He pressed her down to the bed, half-covering her with his weight, his mouth still clamped to hers in a hungry kiss that spoke of a man only just holding on to control. How could she ever have thought she could resist him? The need he stirred in her was almost frightening. It was like a storm rampaging through her flesh—a storm of need and aching want that begged to be assuaged no matter what the consequences.

Matteo lifted his mouth off hers to blaze a trail of red-hot kisses down her neck, his lips moving against her sensitive skin, sending a shower of shivers down her spine. 'I want you so badly.' His voice was a low, primal growl of male need that sent her heart rate soaring.

'I want you too.' Emmie could barely speak louder than a whisper, so intense was her need to feel his possession.

He peeled away her wrap and slid a hand under the V-neck of her nightgown to access her naked breast, his touch sending her into raptures. Her nipple hardened like a pebble, her skin tingling as his warm hand cupped her breast. He bent his head and kissed the skin of her upper breast, his tongue moving against her in a teasing flicker that made her back arch off the bed. He took her nipple in his mouth, teasing it with his tongue, sending sparks of fire through her tender flesh. 'So beautiful…' His voice was sexily husky, his teeth grazing her skin as he moved to her other breast, subjecting it to the same exquisite torture.

Emmie stroked a hand down the marble-hard muscles of his chest and abdomen, her heart thudding like a tribal drum. She could already feel the rise of him against her thigh and desperately wanted to touch him. He made a growling sound of pleasure and it emboldened her to pull away the sheet that was draped over his hips. She took him in her hand and gazed down at his magnificence, her own body preparing in its secretive, sensual way. The liquid dew of arousal formed between her thighs, a persistent throb of want that intensified with each heart-stopping moment. 'You're so…so big…' Her voice caught as another frantic wave of longing swept through her.

Matteo cupped her cheek in his hand, his

gaze locking on hers. 'I won't hurt you. I'll go slowly.'

Emmie stroked her hand down his length again. 'I don't want you to go slowly. I was ready for you ten minutes ago.'

He smiled against her mouth. 'I was ready the moment I met you.'

'Really?'

'Really.' He pressed a hard kiss to her lips and she opened to him, and the kiss deepened, softened and then became urgent once more. He lifted his mouth off hers after a heady moment or two. 'You felt it too that day, didn't you?'

How could she deny it while she was lying in his arms with her body on fire? 'You certainly got my attention, being so demanding and all.' Emmie adopted a playfully reprimanding tone. 'Most of my clients make appointments to see me. They don't barge in insisting on seeing me right then and there.'

His smile was crooked, his eyes gleaming with desire. 'Am I forgiven?'

'Not unless you make love to me right this minute.'

'Now who is being demanding?' His tone was teasing and his smile made her blood sing. His mouth came back down on hers and she was swept away on a tide of longing that thrummed deep and low in her body.

He peeled back her wrap to expose more of her flesh to his hungry gaze. Under any other circumstances, Emmie would have been shy. She would have snatched at the edges of the wrap and tried to cover herself, thinking her curves too small to incite lust in a man. But, with Matteo, she felt gloriously desirable and delighted in watching his smouldering gaze sweep over her as if she was the most beautiful woman he had ever held in his arms.

He kissed his way across her décolletage, his tongue tracing the delicate scaffold of her collar bone and dipping into the shallow dish between it. Emmie shivered under his caresses, her spine tingling in anticipation, her feminine core pulsating with need. Matteo lifted the hem of her nightgown and she wriggled out of it, hauling it over her head and tossing it over the side of the bed.

He ran his gaze over every inch of her and she wondered again why she wasn't shrinking away from him in embarrassment. 'So beautiful…' His voice was a caress in itself, its low rumble rolling down her spine.

'I was thinking the same about you.' Emmie

stroked his hard length with her hand and watched as his face contorted with pleasure.

His hand came over hers to still her caress, his expression sober. 'You're using a reliable contraception?'

The question blind-sided her for a moment. Contraception was something she never had to think about. 'Erm…yes, of course. Completely and utterly reliable.' Emmie figured her damaged ovaries counted much the same as any contraceptive.

Matteo reached for a condom in the bedside drawer and she watched in breathless excitement as he applied it. He came back to her and stroked a lazy hand down the length of her thigh. She quivered under his touch, her need for him so intense it vibrated like a plucked cello string deep in her core. She instinctively opened her thighs, but he didn't respond to her invitation in the way she'd expected. Instead, he moved down her body with a hot trail of kisses from her breasts to her abdomen and then to her feminine mound.

She sucked in a breath and grasped him by the head. 'I haven't let anyone do this before…'

'Relax. Let me be the first then to pleasure you.'

Emmie gave a gulping swallow. She'd had

fantasies about this sort of scenario but never had she thought she would have the courage to allow herself to be so vulnerable. But somehow with Matteo it felt as natural as taking her next breath. She sighed with delight as his mouth came in contact with her swollen flesh, his touch gentle, worshipful, respectful, and her senses went haywire. Tension grew in her tissues, cords of tension that travelled throughout her pelvis in tingling pathways that set her body on fire. His tongue flickered against the tight pearl of her womanhood, the central trigger of female pleasure.

And, suddenly, the storm broke and she was swept up in a vortex of ecstasy that roared, rippled and rumbled through her body. Emmie was shaken to the core by the waves of release that pounded in her flesh, a mind-blowing release that was beyond anything she had ever imagined let alone experienced. It stunned her into silence, only the sound of her heavy breathing audible in the room.

Matteo moved back up her body to kiss her on the lips. She tasted her own essence and was a little shocked at the sheer intimacy of the moment. 'You enjoyed that?' he asked with a knowing smile that set her pulse racing all over again.

Emmie could feel her cheeks growing warm. 'It was beyond anything I've experienced before.'

He brushed a wayward strand of hair back from her face. 'I'm not done with you yet.'

A shiver coursed down her spine at the dark intensity of his gaze. 'Oh, really?'

'Yes, really.' And his mouth came back down on hers like molten fire.

CHAPTER EIGHT

MATTEO HAD MADE love to many women over the course of his adult life, but none had stirred his senses quite like Emmie Woodcroft.

Waking to find her sitting on his bed had turned his nightmare into a dream he knew he wouldn't mind revisiting every night. Her taste was on his tongue, her touch lighting fires over every inch of his skin, his need for her a pounding ache in his groin. He stroked the slim length of her thigh as he deepened his kiss, delighting in the way she whimpered in encouragement. Her legs were tangled with his, her hands playing with his hair in little tugs and caresses that sent tingles racing down the backs of his legs.

'Don't make me wait any longer...' she whispered the words against his lips.

Matteo needed no other inducement and he parted her folds and entered her with a deep groan of pleasure as her slender body gripped him like a fist. He tried to go slowly but her gasps and movements of approval made holding back impossible. He drove into her with increasing speed, going deeper, harder, the primal lust taking control of him like never before. Sensations rippled through him, the delicious friction of her body driving him wild.

He slipped a hand between their rocking bodies, wanting to share this moment of pleasure with her. She was wet, swollen and sweetly fragrant and his senses were intoxicated, drugged, dazed by her. She gave a whimpering cry and arched back sinuously, like a cat, her body quaking, shaking with release. Matteo knew he couldn't hold on much longer. Her body was triggering his with its rippling contractions around him.

He snatched in a breath and then expelled it in a harsh-sounding groan as he finally let go, his scalp tingling, his spine melting, his body shuddering from head to foot with the earth-shattering, planet-spinning pleasure that rocked through him.

Matteo slumped over Emmie in the aftermath, his breathing still ragged, his senses still spinning from a passionate encounter unlike any he'd had before. It was physical pleasure at its finest and, although he'd had plenty of sexual pleasure in the past, something about making love with Emmie had taken it to a whole new level of enjoyment. The cynic in him wanted to point out he hadn't had a lover for a couple of months. His father's death and Matteo's stress over the terms of the will had not exactly been a climate in which to seek a casual lover.

And that was all Emmie wanted to be—a casual lover. The sort of lover he had only ever sought and the sort of lover she only wanted to be—or so she said.

But another less cynical part of him wanted to understand why this encounter with Emmie had been so off-the-charts fantastic. What was it about her that spoke to his flesh and made it wild with lust unlike any he had felt before? Was it simply that breaking his recent sex drought had upped the impact on his senses?

Emmie's hands stroked over his back and shoulders and Matteo shivered in reaction. Her touch was like silk against his skin, soft and gentle, and yet it created a tumult of sensation in his flesh. Electric sensation that made him want her all over again.

Matteo eased away from her to dispose of the condom and then came back and propped himself up on one elbow, gazing down into her pleasure-riven features. 'You left me speechless,' he said with a wry smile.

Her periwinkle-blue eyes sparkled. 'Well, that's only fair, since you did the same to me.'

Matteo trailed a lazy finger down between her breasts. 'When was the last time you had a lover?'

Twin spots of colour bloomed on her cheeks and her smile faded, her gaze lowering to stare at the juncture of his collar bone. 'Why are you asking?' A note of self-doubt crept into her voice. 'Did I act like a novice or something?'

He tipped up her chin to mesh her gaze with his. 'No, not at all. I just wondered, that's all.'

'How long since *you* slept with someone?' She threw his question back at him with a challenging light in her eyes.

'Couple of months.' He didn't tell her the rest—that since his wife and child had died his forays into casual dating hadn't started until a full year after Abriana's death, and only sporadically since then.

Emmie ran the tip of her tongue across her lips and her gaze fell away again from his. 'Well, I've had a bit longer between drinks, so to speak.'

'How long?'

Her teeth began to chew her lower lip. 'I'm too embarrassed to say…'

He bumped up her chin again, locking his gaze on hers. 'Don't be.'

Emmie gave a self-deprecating grimace. 'I haven't had sex since I was a teenager.'

Matteo went completely and utterly still. It was as if every muscle and sinew in his body had been snap frozen. Not since she was a teenager? How could that be? She was an attractive young woman with the same sexual needs as any full-blooded man. Had something happened to her? A sexual assault? Rape? The possible scenarios were ugly, and his gut roiled at the thought of someone abusing her. 'But why on earth not? Did you have a bad experience? Did someone hurt you or…?'

She picked at the edge of the sheet with her fingers, her gaze seemingly unwilling to stay connected to his. 'After I came out of hospital, I felt completely out of step with my peers. I'd stared down death, faced my mortality and dealt with issues most people only face decades later. I couldn't relate to my friends any more. The guys seemed so immature to me, like boys instead of young adult men. The girls weren't much better, although to be fair a couple of friends tried hard to relate to me, but with all the stuff going on at home with my parents and my sister... It...it got too difficult...'

Emmie brought her gaze back up to his and continued, 'I decided to concentrate on my business instead. The only dates I was interested in were other people's. I didn't consider myself a very sexual person until...' Her cheeks were tinged with a faint shade of pink.

'Until now?' he offered.

Emmie gave a wry smile. 'Yes, well, you do have a way of making a girl feel pretty amazing, but no doubt that's because you've had loads and loads of practice.'

Matteo coiled a strand of her silky hair around his finger. 'Sex is not always this good.'

Her eyebrows rose ever so slightly. 'Are you saying you found it amazing too? I mean, more amazing than usual?'

'Why are you so surprised?'

She gave a shrug of one slim shoulder. 'I just thought... I don't know... I've just never seen myself as the sort of woman a man would feel particularly attracted to. Or at least, not enough to have earth-shattering sex with.'

Matteo pressed a brief kiss to her soft mouth. 'I've been fighting my attraction to you from the moment I met you.'

A smile flickered across her lips but it didn't travel the full distance to her eyes. 'That's not going to help your mission to find a wife, though, is it? I'm a distraction you don't really need right now.'

'Maybe I want to be distracted.' Matteo brought his mouth to the side of her neck where her skin was soft and fragrant, sending his senses into mayhem. Would he ever forget the fragrance of her skin? The soft silk of her body lying against his? The hot, tight grip of her feminine muscles around him?

'Maybe I want to forget all about my father's will and enjoy this moment instead.' Matteo wasn't a live-in-the-moment person by nature. He was organised, a planner, his time was structured and never a minute wasted.

But right now, all he wanted was to forget about the clock ticking on the timeline of his father's will and indulge his senses with the most responsive lover he had ever bedded. Besides, his plan to suggest Emmie become the wife he needed was still in place. He was biding his time—the little time he had—because he wanted to wait until he was sure she would say yes.

Emmie murmured under his caresses, her slim body moving against his with enthusiasm. 'I think you're the one doing the distracting,' she said with a breathless sigh as he placed his mouth to her soft breast. 'I can't think straight when you do that.'

'I don't want you to think,' Matteo said, rolling his tongue across her tightly budded nipple. 'I want you to feel.' He circled his tongue around her nipple and then gently took it between the soft press of his teeth. She gave a soft moan and ran her hands down his abdomen to caress his erection. Hot, dark need thundered through his flesh, a need so intense it made every cell in his body throb.

And then, it was Matteo who couldn't think straight. Primal desire drove every thought out of his mind and he gave himself up to the sensual heaven of her touch…

Emmie woke early with one of Matteo's arms flung across her tummy. He was soundly asleep, his hair tousled from where her fingers had clawed through it last night in the throes of mind-blowing sex. She gazed at him for a long moment, memorising every feature of his face. The dark shadow of stubble that was sprinkled across his jaw and around his nose and mouth. The leanness of his face. The chiselled jaw bone. The prominent eyebrows and the permanent trench between them that, right now, was not quite as deep. In sleep he looked more relaxed, younger, less serious, less burdened.

As much as Emmie longed to reach out and stroke him awake, she kept her hands to herself. She knew she had crossed a line by sleeping with him and, while she could never regret the experience of making love with him, she had a job to do, and indulging in a fling was not going to achieve anything but waste his valuable time. Not to mention stirring up a host of longings she had locked away many years ago. But those longings would have to shut the hell up and get back into the vault she had constructed for them and stay there.

Emmie carefully eased out of the bed and slipped on her wrap but in her effort and haste not to wake Matteo, she was unable to find her nightgown. She went back to her own room to give herself a moment to reflect on what had happened during the night. She straightened her barely slept in bed, fussing over the pillows, tempted beyond measure to go back to Matteo's room and enjoy the magic of spending more time in bed with him. But when she reached down to unplug her phone from the charger by the bed she noticed a text message from her mother.

Natty back in hospital.

Emmie's heart sank and guilt washed over her. Her sister's illness was a reminder of how much suffering her own illness had caused to her family and it only reinforced her decision to steer clear of intimate relationships.

And, as timely reminders went, it was certainly bang on time.

Emmie quickly typed a message back, assuring her mother she would be back as soon as she could to offer support. The same support she had been offering for years—hoping, praying, that this time Natty would move a step closer to conquering her illness. The mortality rate from anorexia was the highest of any other mental disorder, a fact that never left Emmie's thoughts. Natty had been in and out of hospital for years, in fact she had spent more time in hospital than Emmie, which seemed ironic under the circumstances.

Ironic and sad, not to mention guilt-inducing.

How could she stay a minute longer with Matteo in Umbria when her sister was fighting for life in hospital? Knowing that, while she was in bed with Matteo Vitale—a client, no less—her mother had been shouldering the burden of her sister's mental health crisis? A crisis that Emmie had caused by becoming ill in the first place. She was doing something she had told herself she never would do—putting her happiness before her family's.

How could she have been so selfish to cross a boundary she had sworn never to cross? Her body still hummed with the pleasure Matteo had evoked. She suspected it would last for days, weeks—maybe for ever. How would she ever forget the magic of his touch? The mind-blowing orgasms that had shaken her from head to toe? The stroke and glide of his hands on her skin, the pressure of his mouth, the taste and texture of his lips, the heat and hardness of his possession?

Emmie slipped her phone in her tote bag and quickly dressed. She left her overnight bag by the door, planning to pick it up once she collected her nightgown from Matteo's room, having only taken her wrap earlier. She told herself it was because she loved that nightgown, it was too expensive to leave behind. But another part of her knew it had more to do with her wanting to see him one more time.

He was still sound asleep and she stood looking at him for a moment or two. Then, with a silent sigh, she bent down to scoop her nightgown off the carpet close to the end of the bed. There was a rustle of bed linen and the sound of Matteo's hand scraping over his stubbled jaw. 'You're up early,' he said. 'Going somewhere?'

Emmie turned to face him, stuffing the nightgown into her tote bag. 'I have to go back to London today.'

His frown deepened and he tossed the sheet aside and stood, and it took every bit of will-power she possessed not to lower her gaze to the perfection of his male body. 'Is something wrong?'

'My sister is unwell. She's been admitted to hospital. I have to get back to support my mother.'

'I'm sorry to hear that.' He stepped into his jeans and zipped them up, then came over and took her by the hands. 'Give me half an hour and I'll come with you.'

Emmie pulled out of his hold. 'No, that's not necessary.' She straightened her tote bag across her shoulder and gave him a tight smile. 'My goal in coming here to see you in your own environment was to get to know you better. I think I've achieved that, and so now I need to get back to the job you're paying me to do. Finding you a wife.'

Matteo's face froze as if every muscle had been paralysed. He stared fixedly at her for a long moment. 'Thank you for taking the trouble to come.' Somehow Emmie suspected there was a double entendre lurking in his curt response.

'Thank you for having me.' Two could play at that game. 'Will you thank Valentina for me? It was a lovely meal last night.' Emmie moved towards the door. 'I just have to get my overnight bag from my room… I've already packed.'

Would the housekeeper be surprised that Emmie hadn't spent the whole night in the room she had prepared for her? Or perhaps Valentina was used to a bit of female-guest bed-hopping. No doubt Emmie wasn't the first woman Matteo had bedded here. He was a virile man in the prime of his life—every intimate muscle in her body could vouch for that.

'I'll take your bag down for you,' Matteo said in a firm tone that quickly dispensed with any notion of her arguing with him.

'Fine. That's…kind of you.'

A short time later, Matteo carried Emmie's bag down to her hire car and placed it in the boot. He knew she had a valid excuse for leaving earlier than he had expected, but it still niggled him that she might have decided to leave early in any case. She had planned to stay three days and was leaving after only one. How could he not feel short-changed, especially after last night? He'd been looking forward to spending more time with her, and not just in bed. There were things he wanted to show her on the estate, and he wanted to tell her some of the history of the place that went back centuries.

He opened the driver's door for her, aching to touch her before she got behind the wheel, but somehow summoning up the self-control not to. The lines of their 'relationship' were blurry enough. Maybe this was the right way to go—let her leave without any hint of regret on his part.

It stirred a memory of the day his mother had left. But back then he had bawled and begged her to stay, his gut had hollowed out, his chest so tight, as if a clamp had been on his ribs, his eyes streaming, nose running, hopes fading. But, of course, his mother had not changed her mind. She had driven away down the driveway without once looking back.

'Drive safely,' Matteo said, closing the door for Emmie.

She started the car and pressed the button to

lower the window. 'I'll be in touch with some potential dates. And I should have your personality profile results back early next week. That will make things a lot easier.'

He arched one eyebrow. 'What? You don't know me well enough by now?' He injected his tone with a hint of mockery.

A flicker of something passed across her face, and then her lips pressed together. 'Thank you again for your hospitality.' Her voice was as polite and formal as a robot's and just as impersonal.

Matteo stepped back from the car and turned back to the villa. He was damned if he was going to watch her drive away.

But he *would* see her again. He would not leave things so up in the air between them, not after last night. Emmie was upset about her sister and needed some time to be with her family. But, once the time was right, he would present her with a proposal she could not possibly refuse.

CHAPTER NINE

EMMIE SAT BY her sister's bedside while a naso-gastric tube fed Natty essential nutrients to keep her organs from failing. Her sister was shockingly thin, little more than a skeleton tightly wrapped in greyish-hued skin, with bruises all over her body, sores where she had been picking at herself, her nails bitten down to the quick.

Emmie fought back tears, her chest so tight she could barely breathe. How could she not feel responsible for the illness that ravaged her younger sister's body and mind? How could she not feel guilty that it was her cancer that had torn apart her family, throwing poor lit-tle Natty into the grip of a deadly condition even more deadly than Emmie's? Over the last couple of months, there had been some im-provement in Natty's condition. Not much im-provement, only a smidgen, but still, anything was better than nothing.

But now this heartbreaking backward step...

It was hard to cling on to hope that her sister would one day turn a corner, that this dreadful illness would somehow lose its grip on her and allow her to live a more normal life. It was so sad to think that, like her, Natty was infertile—not from chemo, but from years of malnutrition, particularly as it had started in young adolescence.

Emmie knew anorexia was a mental health condition, that Natty's starved brain caused the disordered thinking that perpetuated her disease. But she was still angry at her sister for not responding to the costly treatment she had been given over the years. Time was running out; her sister's ravaged body could not take too much more. It intensified Emmie's feelings of powerless and guilt for her part in her sister's illness.

Their mother, Gwen, sat on the other side of the hospital bed, looking a decade older than she should. Her blonde hair was streaked with grey, her skin was sallow, her eyes hollow with dark circles below and there were deep lines on her face that hadn't been there the last time Emmie had seen her.

'Has Dad been in yet?' Emmie asked in a low voice.

Her mother shook her head, her shoulders slumping. 'You know what he's like. He finds hospitals too upsetting.' The disdain in her voice was unmistakable. 'And do you think I don't too? But here I am, week after week, month after month, year after year, wondering if it will ever come to an end.' Gwen brushed at her eyes with the back of her hand, her chin trembling as she fought back tears.

Emmie came round the other side of the bed and knelt down beside her mother's chair. She took her mother's hands in her own and gently stroked them. 'Oh, Mum, you've had to deal with so much pain and stress, it's so unfair.'

Her mother sniffed and looked at Emmie through watery eyes. 'Do you think it's my fault? I wasn't a good enough mother?'

'Stop it,' Emmie said, squeezing her mother's hands. 'You heard what the psychologist said during that session we had. That mother-blaming stuff was what they thought in the past, but they don't now. It's a mental illness and not at all your fault.'

Gwen sighed so deeply, her shoulders went down another notch. 'It's hard not to blame myself when both my daughters have been so ill. I keep thinking I must have done something wrong during my pregnancies. Was it something I ate or drank? Chemicals I consumed in processed food? Not enough exercise? Too much? The guilt never goes away.'

Tell me about it.

Emmie had been accompanied by guilt every day of her life since her diagnosis. Had she done something that had caused her cancer? Had that one cigarette she'd tried when she was fourteen triggered rogue cancer cells in her body? Had the sip or two of vodka at a party when she was sixteen done it?

The one thing she did know was that her illness had caused unbearable stress to her parents and in consequence her sister. Natty hadn't coped with the long absences of their mother during Emmie's hospital stays. She hadn't coped with their father's emotional distance, or his constant criticism over her not doing her homework or her chores. It had been too much for quiet, overly sensitive Natty, whose life had spun so quickly out of control that she'd controlled the only thing she could—her eating.

'I guess that's how most loving mothers would feel...' Emmie said. Not that she would ever know that feeling now. Motherhood was an impossible dream, a shattered dream. She would never have a child of her own. IVF with a donor egg was an option but she would never see aspects of herself or her sister or parents in a tiny baby's face in the way biological parents did.

Gwen grasped Emmie's hand. 'Darling, thank you for being with me. But you said you were in Italy. What for? You never mentioned going on holiday when we spoke a couple of weeks ago.'

'It wasn't a holiday. I went for work.'

Her mother looked at her expectantly, obviously wanting more information. Emmie was reluctant to give too much away. There was client confidentiality, for one thing, and then there was the agreement between her and Matteo that what happened in Umbria stayed in Umbria. But as long as she didn't reveal his name, Emmie comforted herself, her mother would never find out who he was.

'I was visiting a client at his villa in Umbria.' Emmie filled in the silence. 'A high-end client. He's in rather a hurry to find himself a wife.'

'Sounds intriguing. What's he like?'

Emmie wondered what her mother would say if she told her that only hours ago she had been in bed with him. That even now she missed him as if a part of her had been left behind in Italy. She had relived every moment of their night together since, her body tingling all over as each erotic scene played out in her mind. 'He's a widower. He lost his wife and baby eight years ago.'

'Oh, how terribly sad.'

'Yes…' Emmie got up from the floor and forced a smile. 'But he's keen to marry again and it's my job to find him a suitable partner.'

Gwen smiled back. 'You bring happiness to so many people, sweetie. I'm so proud of you.'

But Emmie wasn't able to bring happiness or healing to her family, and that plagued her constantly. Her parents were bitter enemies, her sister was creeping closer and closer to death's door and Emmie was unable to do anything to help.

'Thanks, Mum.' Emmie bent down to drop a kiss on the top of her mother's head. 'I'm proud of you too.'

A few days later, Emmie finally got the results of Matteo's personality profile. It didn't reveal much more than she had already surmised. He was a man who preferred his own company to that of others. He was goal-and achievement-oriented and he had strong personal values. He thought before he spoke, he reflected before he acted, he was not driven by emotions but by logic. He sought organisation and efficiency, and took pride in doing any job he set out to do and doing it to the best of his ability. But he wasn't without sensitivity and emotional intelligence—the feedback showed a broad band of those qualities, although it wasn't his primary strength.

Emmie went back through her database and selected the female clients she thought would be most suitable for him. She ended up with four on her shortlist but she felt none of her normal excitement about finding a match for a client. In fact, she was jealous that someone else would experience the passionate press of his lips on theirs. Someone else would experience the magic of being in his arms, the mind-blowing magic of making love with him.

Jealousy was an emotion she had never experienced before, or at least not in this context. Sure, she was jealous when she saw young women pushing prams, or stroking their bulging tummies during pregnancy. How could she not be envious of a state that fate had decided she would never experience? Every time she saw a baby or a young child, her heart would ache as if it had been pierced with an arrow.

Several of her happily married clients had come in with their new babies and Emmie had cuddled and cooed over those precious little bundles, displaying an acting ability that was worthy of an award. No one would ever guess how gut-wrenching it was for her to smell a new-born's beautiful smell, to look down into their little, scrunched-up pixie faces, to listen to their cute little snuffles and sighing noises, knowing she would never give birth to her own child.

Emmie reached for her phone to call Matteo and organise some potential dates but, just then, Paisley popped her head round the door.

'Guess who's come to see you?' She waggled her eyebrows and added, 'Your favourite client.'

Emmie's heart stumbled like a foot missing a bottom step. 'He's not my favourite but he's certainly my most difficult.' Difficult to resist, difficult to forget, difficult to put out of her mind. She had replayed their night together so many times, her body aching for him like it had never ached before. He had triggered desires and needs in her she had no way of satisfying now. Not without him. Self-pleasure was an option, of course, but it would be a paltry substitute now she had experienced the explosive fire of his touch.

Matteo entered her office a moment or two later, his dark-blue gaze meeting hers. 'How is your sister?'

'A little better, thank you.' Natty had marginally improved now that she'd had some intravenous nutrition, but how long she would stay that way once she went home was anyone's guess.

'Still in hospital?'

'Yes, she will be for another week or so.' Emmie waved at the chair in front of her desk. 'Please, sit down. I was about to contact you with some potential dates now that I've read your personality profile. You received a copy of the report via email?'

'*Si.*'

'Did anything surprise you in it? Anything you didn't already know about yourself?'

'No.'

Emmie forced a stiff smile. 'A lot of my clients are quite surprised. They find it helpful to understand how they come across, what personality traits or ways of relating to people might be getting in the way of them finding a partner—that sort of thing.'

'Have you had yours done?' His gaze was unwavering on hers.

'Yes, as a matter of fact I have.'

'And?'

Emmie moistened her suddenly parchment-dry lips, the penetrating beam of his gaze making her feel as if she were under a microscope. Could he see how much his presence stirred her senses into overdrive? Could he sense how hard and fast her pulse was beating? 'And what?'

'Were you surprised by what you found out about your personality?'

'Yes and no.'

A lazy smile tilted his mouth. 'Let me guess what it said.'

She pressed her spine more firmly back into her chair, desperately trying not to look at his mouth. The mouth that had kissed hers and set it on fire, leaving smouldering embers in her body that his mere presence now fanned into leaping flames. 'Go ahead.'

His chair creaked as he changed position, one ankle crossing over his bent knee in a relaxed pose. 'You're warm and compassionate and like helping people. You rely on your gut rather than your head when you decide about something. How am I doing so far?'

'Not bad.' Rather brilliantly, actually. But there were things he could never know about her and she was going to keep it that way.

His smile broadened and her heart tripped and flipped. 'You're observant and dedicated with strong personal values. You don't enjoy the company of people who show little regard for other's feelings.' His eyes darkened and his gaze dipped to her mouth before he added in a deeper, huskier tone, 'You're a very sensual person, passionate and fiery, although you try to hide it.'

Emmie tried to ignore the hot flutter of desire between her thighs, tried to ignore the way her lips were tingling, aching to feel his mouth upon them. She pushed back her chair and stood, folding her arms across her chest, fixing him with a cool stare. 'Mr Vitale, I think—'

'Mr?' His dark eyebrows rose cynically and he stood from his chair and strode over to where she was standing. 'Surely, after our time in Umbria, we have moved past such formalities, *si*?'

His deep baritone was a caress that glided down her spine and left a warm pool of longing in its wake.

Emmie had plenty of time to move out of his reach but found herself unable to move a muscle. She was spellbound by the glint in his eyes, mesmerised by the sensual energy that passed like a current between their bodies. Her gaze drifted to his mouth and her stomach swooped and her pulse raced. She caught the citrus notes of his aftershave, the sharp lemon and lime drugging her senses. 'We agreed that what h-happened in Umbria stayed in Umbria. We—we need to forget about it and move on.' Her voice wasn't as steady as she'd hoped, and nor was her heartbeat—it was going at a hit-and-miss pace.

Matteo placed a gentle finger beneath her chin and lifted her face so her eyes meshed with his. He was close enough for her to see the black, bottomless depths of his pupils and the tiny flecks of different shades of blue that made his irises look like a mysterious labyrinth. 'I haven't forgotten a moment.' His thumb began a slow stroke of her lower lip, setting every nerve in her mouth on fire.

Emmie tried to disguise a gulping swallow but the sound was clearly audible. 'It shouldn't have happened. *I* shouldn't have let it happen.'

His brows snapped together. 'You regret it?'

She chewed at one edge of her mouth. How could she regret the most amazing experience of her life? It was right up there with the day she'd been declared cancer-free. But how could she allow herself to take it any further? It would be stepping outside the parameters she had set for herself. Other people's happiness was her business now, not seeking her own. 'No. I don't. It was…wonderful, amazing, unforgettable…but it can't happen again.'

'Why can't it?'

Emmie's brain was scrambled by his proximity, addled by his touch, dazed by the desire she could see gleaming in his eyes. She was *supposed* to be able to resist him. She was *supposed* to avoid tricky emotional entanglements, because that was the only way to appease the guilt she carried around how her cancer had ruined her once-happy family. But as soon as Matteo stepped into her presence a tidal wave of longing swept her up and carried her into a fantasy world where she promised herself, *just one more time*.

'You know why not.'

He held her gaze for a long, throbbing moment. 'Let's pretend I'm not a client right now. Just for a couple of days—a week.'

'But you don't have time to waste and—'

'I can afford a week or two.' His hands came down to settle on her hips, bringing her closer to the tall, hard frame of his body. The body that had possessed her and thrilled her and was now making it hard—nay, impossible—for her to rustle up the willpower to say no.

'You mean...continue our fling?'

His finger stroked from her ear to the bottom of her chin in a caress that made every knob of her spine shiver in reaction. 'I want you.' His statement was blunt, bold, and it spoke to every cell in her flesh, causing her to vibrate with desire deep and low in her core. 'And I know you want me.' He brought her even closer, his body so hard against her belly she almost came on the spot.

Emmie drew in a rattling breath and released it in a shuddering stream. 'I don't suppose there's any point in me denying it?'

His smile was knowing, his gaze glinting. 'I could kiss you right now and prove it.' His gaze lowered to her mouth and her heart leapt in anticipation. 'But I'm going to make you wait until tonight.'

Disappointment flooded through her. He was going to make her *wait*? Tonight was hours away. 'Tonight? What's happening tonight?'

He stroked a slow-moving finger across her tingling mouth, the top lip and then the lower one, ramping up her need for him with every sexy graze of his finger. His gaze was still as dark as a midnight sky, the sparks of male desire like winking stars from an outer galaxy. 'I think you know what's going to happen.' He dropped his hand from her face and stepped back. 'I'll pick you up at eight. Bring a toothbrush and a change of clothes.'

Emmie arched one eyebrow. 'What about a nightgown?'

He gave her a smouldering look that made every intimate muscle in her body fizz like shaken champagne. 'You won't need it.' And, without another word, he left.

Matteo had to stop himself from turning up at Emmie's house an hour earlier than he'd said. Anticipation thundered through his blood, the need to make love to her again driving every other thought out of his head. He knew he was acting out of character by putting to one side his mission to fulfil the terms of his father's will, but he was compelled to explore the blistering sensuality between himself and Emmie Woodcroft. How he had stopped himself from kissing her in her office earlier today still surprised him. Who knew he had such iron-clad self-control? She had tested it, though, tested it almost beyond its endurance.

Emmie was the most alluring woman he had ever met and the thought of making love to her again made him ache and pound with need. He was unable to get the memory of their passionate lovemaking out of his mind. It was the first thing he thought of when he woke, the last thing he thought of before he slept, and it filled his thoughts throughout the day. He was a man obsessed and he had to get control of it otherwise he was going to lose even more valuable time.

Matteo was determined not to fall in love, but he had nothing against having a short fling with Emmie in order to convince her to consider his proposal, because the combustible chemistry between them was beyond anything he had experienced before.

They had only had one night together and that wasn't enough. No way was it enough. The disappointment he'd felt when she'd left him that day at his villa had made him all the more determined to see her again. She had stirred a bone-deep longing in him that was making it difficult to think about anything but making love to her again.

But he was acutely aware of the time frame

in his father's will that added a whole other level of urgency to his relationship with Emmie. One that was impossible to ignore.

CHAPTER TEN

EMMIE OPENED THE door to Matteo right on the dot of eight p.m. 'Hi.' She was strangely tongue-tied, feeling as shy as a girl going on her first date. 'I—I just have to get my toiletries bag. Make yourself at home and...'

Matteo stepped over the threshold and closed the door, taking her by the upper arms before she could step away to collect her things. He brought his mouth down on hers in a blistering kiss that lifted every hair on her head and sent sparks of electricity shooting through her blood. His tongue entered her mouth in a bold thrust that had distinctly erotic overtones, the flickers and darts of tongue-play making every female hormone in her body do a happy dance, like an over-pumped cheerleading squad. His hands moved from her upper arms to glide down to her hips, bringing her closer to the proud jut of his arousal. Desire flooded her being, dousing her in molten flames of lust that licked at every inch of her flesh.

He finally lifted his mouth off hers and gave one of his crooked smiles. 'I would have done that earlier today, but I wasn't sure your receptionist would be able to handle it if she happened to come in on us having red-hot sex on your desk.'

Emmie licked the salty taste of his lips from her own, a frisson passing over her body at the sexy scene he had just planted in her mind. 'I'm not sure I would have been able to handle it either. Desk sex sounds a little uncomfortable.'

His eyes smouldered. 'I'd make sure it wasn't.'

That she could well believe. Emmie linked her arms around his neck and planted a soft kiss to his lips. 'I'll hold you to that some time but not here. The desk I have in my home office is an heirloom ladies' writing desk that used to belong to my great-grandmother. She would probably spin in her grave if I used it in such a way.'

Matteo smiled and placed his hands on the curve of her bottom, his hardened length stirring her female flesh into a madcap frenzy. His mouth came back down to just above hers.

'Do you know how crazy with desire you make me? I can't think of anything but how much I want to be inside you again.'

Emmie gave an involuntary shudder, her body already hot and damp with desire. 'You drive me more than a little crazy too.'

He closed the distance between their mouths, his lips moulding to hers in a mind-altering kiss that swept her up into a vortex of thundering longing. Need pulsated throughout her lower body, a desperate, clawing need that made her feel hollow and empty without his thick, hard presence. Now that she had experienced his possession, her body craved it like a drug. Needed to feel the ecstasy of his earth-shattering lovemaking.

Matteo placed one hand in the small of her back and the other slipped up behind her head, his fingers tangling in her hair, sending shivers cascading down her spine. His kiss became more urgent, more intense, more spellbinding. Emmie groaned against his mouth, delighting in the hard pressure that signalled his desperate need for her—the same need that was consuming her.

Matteo finally tore his mouth away, his breathing heavy, his eyes shining brightly with unbridled lust. 'As much as I'd like to finish this here and now, I have a special evening planned for you.' He gave a rueful twist of his mouth and added, 'Besides, I'm mussing up your hair and make-up and giving you beard rash.' He touched a gentle finger to her chin.

What could be more special than being ravished inside her front doorway? Never had such thrilling excitement thundered through her blood. Never had she experienced such giddy anticipation. 'I gotta admire your self-control,' Emmie said. 'It's a whole lot better than mine.'

Matteo smiled and brushed her cheek with his bent knuckles in a light-as-air caress. 'Go and get your things. I'll wait for you here.'

Emmie scooted away to get her toiletries bag, her heart still thudding like a mad thing in her chest, her lips still tingling from his kiss, desire still pounding in her body. She caught a glimpse of herself in her bathroom mirror and was a little shocked at what she saw reflected back at her. Her hair was tousled where Matteo's hands had played with it, her eyes were bright as headlamps and her lips were swollen, without the coating of lip-gloss she had applied earlier that evening. And there was a reddened patch on her chin where his stubble had grazed her. She touched it with her finger, her stomach freefalling at the thought of his stubbly face buried between her thighs.

Emmie took a breath and released it in a shuddering stream. She had not thought it possible to be so madly attracted to a man that nothing else would matter other than getting naked with him as soon as humanly possible. If anyone had told her even a couple of weeks ago that she would be in such a giddy state of arousal, she would have rolled about the floor laughing. But now all she could think about was rolling around a bed, a floor and, yes, even a desk with Matteo Vitale.

And the sooner, the better.

A short while later, Matteo led Emmie into the restaurant he'd booked in Mayfair. He had been in two minds over whether to skip dinner altogether and go straight back to his house and make passionate love to her. But he wanted this evening to be special because he'd been thinking about her lack of dating experience.

He wasn't sure how he felt about being her first lover since she'd been a teenager. Honoured? Privileged? Touched? None of those words adequately summed up how he felt. He mostly dated women with loads of experience, so it was certainly a novel experience to sleep with someone who was practically a virgin. He was used to worldly women who played the same game as him—casual dates with no-strings sex.

Emmie was hardly worldly, but she wasn't unsophisticated. She was naturally elegant, and poised and articulate. And, while she hadn't had a lot of sexual experience, he would never have guessed from her responses to him. She responded with such enthusiasm, receiving him as if her body had been designed especially for him and his for her.

The more time he spent with her, the more he longed to know about her. Emmie was the first woman he had wanted to get to know on a deeper level. His relationships in the past had been short, some might even go as far to describe them as shallow. Even his relationship with his late wife had hardly been what anyone could call close. It had been a convenient solution to marry for the sake of their surprise pregnancy.

It saddened him that he had been unable to return Abriana's feelings for him. She had deserved better, but how could he have given her what he hadn't had? His ability to form a deep and loving attachment had no doubt been blighted by the walk-out of his mother when he'd been such a young age. Which was why he had been so careful not to raise anyone's expectations in relationships since.

Matteo cupped Emmie's elbow as they made their way to their table. Her petite frame brushed against him. The flowery notes of her perfume drifted past his nostrils and a wave of desire washed over him in a hot tide. She glanced up at him with a small smile and he fantasised about kissing her soft lips again. She had covered the beard rash with some make-up but just knowing it was still there made his groin tighten.

'Here we go.' He pulled out a chair for her and waited for her to be seated. He rested his hands on the tops of her shoulders for a moment before going to his own chair opposite.

'This is nice,' Emmie said, glancing round at the other tables which were situated some distance from theirs. 'Oh, there's a dance floor...' Her teeth sank into her lower lip.

'You like dancing?'

Her cheeks grew pink and she made a business of spreading her napkin over her lap, her gaze not quite meeting his. 'I love it but I'm hopeless at it. I'd have to be tipsy to get on a dance floor and, since I don't drink, that's not going to happen any time soon.'

'Did you ever drink alcohol?'

'If you can call having a sip or two of vodka at a party when I was sixteen drinking, then yes, I used to.'

'But nothing since?'

She shook her head. 'I don't mind other people drinking in moderation but it's not for me.' She waited a beat and added in an altered tone, 'I'm too scared…'

'Of making a fool of yourself?'

Emmie met his gaze with a sombre one. 'Of getting cancer.'

A knife-like pain suddenly hit him in the chest. *Emmie was terrified of getting cancer again.*

He could only imagine how hard it would be to live with the threat of it hanging over her. He knew about the carcinogenic properties of excessive alcohol use and that even drinking in moderation contained some element of risk. He was a moderate drinker himself. He hadn't been drunk or even tipsy since he'd been a teenager, and even then, it had only been the once. He admired her stance. It showed discipline and the ability to resist peer pressure. But it also showed how much her cancer diagnosis had impacted her. 'It sounds like you made the right choice, then.'

'Yes. I don't ever want to go through chemo again. It was ghastly.' She gave a little shudder and picked up her glass of water. 'Let's talk about something else. I hate thinking about that time in my life.'

'But in a way, it's made you who you are today.'

'Yes, but I often wonder who I might have been if I hadn't got sick,' Emmie said, frowning slightly as she looked at the ice cubes in her glass. 'And if my parents wouldn't have split up and my sister get an eating disorder.' She glanced up at him and asked, 'Do you ever wonder what you would be like now if your mother hadn't left when she did?'

Matteo gave a one-shoulder shrug. 'Who knows?'

'Do you think it's affected you in any way?'

'A bit, perhaps.'

'Do you want to know what I think?' Emmie asked, and without waiting for him to answer continued, 'You find emotional intimacy difficult because you were abandoned as a young child by a primary carer. And, since your father struggled when your mother left, you taught yourself to be independent and emotionally distant. But you can train yourself to be more open emotionally. It's hard, but it can be done. Otherwise relationships, particularly intimate ones, will always be fraught with difficulty.'

'But what if I don't want that sort of relationship?' Matteo said with a cynical smile. 'What if I'm perfectly happy with being independent and emotionally distant?'

'But you're not.'

Matteo arched an eyebrow. 'So you believe, but you've only known me a week or so.'

'Maybe, but I'm pretty good at reading people.'

'So…' He glanced at her mouth before meeting her gaze once more. 'Tell me what I'm thinking right at this very moment.'

Emmie's cheeks went a deeper shade of pink. 'You're uncomfortable with my line of questioning, so you're trying to distract me.'

'And how I am distracting you, hmm?'

'By looking at me as if you want to forget about dinner and go straight to your place and have mind-blowing sex. Am I right?'

Matteo smiled. 'You're good.'

Emmie smiled back. 'It's how I make my living.' Her smile slowly faded, her gaze fell away, and she began to make a circular pattern with her fingertip on the tablecloth near her glass. 'I've made a shortlist of candidates for you to—'

'I thought we agreed to forget about that for the next few days?' Matteo asked. The thought of dating anyone else while he was indulging in a fling with Emmie seemed a little weird, if not downright distasteful. He couldn't imagine wanting to talk to another woman, let alone date anyone else. Nor did he want his so-called fling with Emmie to be over any time soon, which was unusual in itself. He was normally formulating an exit strategy on the second date. But not with Emmie.

'Fine but, given the time pressure, I need to have a plan in place. It takes time to get to know someone and—'

'Not according to what you said a few moments ago,' Matteo said with a sardonic look. 'You claim to know everything about me and we only met less than a fortnight ago.'

'Yes, but that's me. Someone else might not have the same ability to see you for who you are. They might be turned off, like Karena Thorsby was, thinking you were intimidating—which you are, by the way.'

'But it doesn't seem to bother you.'

She shrugged and gave him a crooked smile. 'You know what I thought when I first met you? You reminded me of a wolf with a wounded paw.'

Matteo held up both his hands. 'As you see, no wounds.'

'You hide your pain because to reveal it to anyone would make you feel too vulnerable. Like a lot of men, you see vulnerability as a weakness, but I see it as a strength. Admitting you haven't got it all together and need the support of others is an admirable quality.' Emmie leaned forward across the table and placed a hand on his chest, right over the top of his heart. She looked directly into his eyes with her own periwinkle-blue ones. 'There's your wound.'

He held her gaze for a long beat, the warmth of her hand seeping into all the cold corners of his chest, threatening to melt the cage of ice around his heart. Or maybe it wasn't the physical touch of her hand that threatened to chip away the thick layer of ice. It was the way she looked at him—*really* looked at him. Emmie wasn't someone who was satisfied with what she saw on the outside. She went deeper, the way he did as a forensic accountant. Looking for discrepancies, looking for clues, looking for things that didn't add up. She had looked at him that way from the very first day, seeing through his emotional armour like a security scanner, somehow intuiting that all was not right in his life.

Over the short time he had known her, he had told her more about himself than he had told anyone and, yes, it did make him feel vulnerable. When she'd stumbled across the graves of his wife and child he had opened up his world of pain to her, and he had been touched that she seemed to understand in a way few people could.

Matteo captured her hand and brought it up to his mouth, pressing a kiss to each of her fingertips. 'And where is your wound, *cara mia*?'

Her eyelids flickered as if his question had momentarily thrown her. 'I—I don't have one.' Her slim throat rose and fell, and even with the background noise of the restaurant he heard the sound of her tight swallow.

Matteo kept hold of her hand, his thumb stroking across the soft skin of her palm. 'Ah, but that is not quite true, is it? We all have some hoof print of hurt from the past, often from some event in our childhood or adolescence. And you've had cancer, which is one hell of a wound to deal with—one, I suspect, that would leave a much larger hoof print than most.'

'But I was cured, so I don't have that wound any more.'

'But you still worry about getting cancer again.'

Her gaze lowered to the collar of his shirt. 'Yes, but so do most cancer survivors. Every ache or pain, you wonder... *Is it back*? Every annual check-up and blood test are an anxiety fest until the results come back normal.'

Her gaze crept back up to his. 'It's a heck of a way to live, but I'm glad I'm still living. There were a couple of other teenagers on the ward with me who didn't make it. I made a promise to myself back then that I would make the most of my life to honour them. And I believe I do that every time I match up two people and they fall in love with each other and get their happy-ever-after. Nothing gives me more pleasure.'

Matteo hooked one eyebrow upwards, his thumb circling her palm in a caressing manner. 'Nothing?'

Emmie's cheeks went pink again and she gave a wry smile. 'Well, apart from *that*.' She paused for a moment and added, 'But I don't regret waiting this long to...to have a fling. I needed to concentrate on my business and it might not have been as successful as it's been if I'd been distracted by my own relationship. An intimate relationship takes time and commitment. I've put that time and commitment into my career.'

'There might be a time when a career isn't enough for you any more.'

Emmie pulled her hand out of his and picked up her water glass, shooting him a look from beneath her lowered lashes. 'Not every woman wants the husband, the kids and the white picket fence, you know.'

'Do your parents pressure you and your sister to give them grandchildren?' Matteo asked, thinking of the endless nagging his father had gone on with over the years, about Matteo producing an heir.

Emmie put her glass back on the table, but seemed to misjudge where the cutlery was. The stem caught the tines of her fork and the glass fell over, spilling water across the tablecloth. 'Oh, shoot. I'm sorry for being so clumsy.' She began to mop up the spill with her napkin but a waiter soon rushed across and took over.

Matteo couldn't help feeling his question had unsettled her and wondered if her parents were the traditional sort who expected their offspring to date, get engaged, marry and then produce children in that order, as they had. He had lived experience of parental pressure, and if anything, it had achieved the opposite, making him even more determined not to settle down. Which was no doubt why his father had gone to the lengths he had to get Matteo to do what he wanted.

The waiter replaced the tablecloth and poured Emmie a fresh glass of water and then discreetly melted away again.

'Will you excuse me?' Emmie said before Matteo could resume the thread of conversation. 'I need to freshen up.'

'Sure.' He watched her weave her way through the tables, a frown deepening on his brow. If her parents had pressured her the way his father had pressured him, then Emmie and he had more in common than he'd thought.

No wonder he felt such a deep connection with her.

CHAPTER ELEVEN

EMMIE WAS GLAD the rest room was empty so she could pull herself together in private. Matteo's question had caught her off-guard, not because she hadn't been asked such a question before—she had, many times, too many times to count. Her parents were the last people who would ever pressure her to produce grandchildren, because they knew she couldn't. Nor could Natty, unless her condition was cured, and unfortunately, with every year that passed, that was looking more and more unlikely.

It pained Emmie every time she saw her mother's wistful glance at a pram or a pregnant woman, or when she walked past a children's wear boutique. Her mother was careful to do it covertly but Emmie had seen it enough times to know her mother grieved deeply for the shattered dream of one day holding her own grandchild in her arms.

It was why Emmie didn't add to her mother's grief by openly expressing her own sadness at not being able to have a baby. She pretended it would have been her choice to be childless regardless of her chemo-induced infertility. What good would it do to dump even more pain on her already overburdened mother? It wouldn't be fair, nor would it achieve anything but inflict more emotional distress. Her cancer had taken so much away from her but it had also stolen so much from her family. The future they had once envisaged, the happiness and healthiness all of them had taken for granted until it was snatched away.

Emmie could no longer be the daughter her parents had once pictured as the mother of their future grandchildren. How, then, could she dare to picture herself as someone suitable for Matteo? It was an impossible dream. A fool's dream.

Emmie finger-combed her hair, reapplied her lip-gloss and took a deep breath to compose herself. Spending time with Matteo Vitale was exciting, exhilarating and erotic, and yet he threatened everything she had worked so hard to finally accept in her life. She knew it was hypocritical of her to call out his fear of vulnerability when she was covering up her own. His laser-like focus, his forensically trained, sharply intelligent mind and his assiduous attention to detail were qualities she deeply admired in him, and yet they were the very qualities that most unsettled her. While she didn't believe vulnerability was a weakness, *her* vulnerability was nobody's business but her own.

And she intended to keep it that way.

The band had taken up position next to the dance floor by the time Emmie got back to the table. Matteo rose from his chair and held out his hands. 'How about we try out those two left feet of yours?'

Emmie fought back a smile. 'Are you wearing steel-toed shoes? Don't say I didn't warn you.'

'I have a high pain threshold.'

Emmie didn't for a moment doubt it. He had lost his wife and child and, while he claimed not to have been in love with Abriana, he most certainly felt enormous guilt and sadness at the loss of her life and that of their child. It struck Emmie then how similar he and she were. Both dealing with deep personal sadness, pretending to everyone they were fine when they were not. They had each buried their sadness and carried on the best way they knew how.

Matteo led her to the dance floor, held her in the waltz position and began moving with her to the slow ballad. Emmie moved with him, a little surprised at how natural it felt, as if they had been dancing together for years. Three other couples joined them but to Emmie it felt as if she and Matteo were completely alone. His hand on the small of her back sent tingles down the backs of her legs. The fingers of his other hand were warm and gentle around hers. His navy-blue eyes held hers in a mesmerising lock, communicating a sensually charged message that made her skin tighten in anticipation.

'You're a natural,' Matteo said, bringing her closer to his body, close enough for her to feel the impact she was having on him. It thrilled her to feel his reaction, the stirring of his body sending a hot wave of desire flooding through hers.

'I don't know about that. Maybe it's because you're such a good partner,' Emmie said, gazing up at him.

His eyes darkened and dipped to her mouth and her heart missed a beat. Her words seemed to ring in the silence. *Such a good partner.* The perfect partner in so many ways. But her job was to *find* him someone, not to be that someone herself.

There was no way anyone could describe her as the perfect partner for him. She could not give him what he most wanted. He didn't want love or even long-term commitment. What he wanted, needed, was an heir. There was no magic wand or benevolent fairy godmother that could ever bring that about for her. Her fate had been decided eight years ago, the day she had first been diagnosed with cancer.

Eight years ago…

And there was another similarity between her and Matteo. Eight years ago, his life had changed for ever when his wife and child had died in a car crash. The same year Emmie had been fighting for her life, his wife and child had lost theirs.

Matteo brought one of his hands to the small frown on Emmie's forehead, smoothing it out with his finger. 'So serious all of a sudden. Is something wrong?' His tone had a note of concern.

Emmie gave a vestige of a smile. 'I was just thinking that eight years ago we were both going through terrible times on opposite sides of the world. It's kind of spooky how two strangers' lives can intersect.'

Matteo brushed his fingers beneath her chin in a feather-light caress. 'Have you heard the saying, "strangers are friends you haven't yet met"?'

'No, but I like it.' She paused for a beat before asking, 'Is that how you see me? As a friend?'

His eyes moved between hers for a pulsing moment, his expression inscrutable. 'That's what you like to be for your clients, isn't it? The friend that facilitates a perfect match for them.'

Emmie sent the tip of her tongue out over her lips. 'Yes, that's exactly what I try to be. Someone they can rely on to be there for them, to help them identify and then push through the emotional barriers that have prevented them from finding love in the past.'

Matteo turned her away from one of the couples who were coming a bit close. His arms around her were strong and protective, the warmth of his body heating every tissue in hers. 'Some people find love only to lose it. My parents, your parents, numerous others.' His tone was more reflective than cynical, merely stating what he had observed.

'I know, and it's often the fear of losing love that prevents people from seeking it again.'

Emmie looked up at him again. 'My mother is a case in point.'

'You haven't tried matching her with anyone?'

'I mentioned it a couple of times but she was pretty adamant she was never going to get involved with anyone ever again.' Emmie sighed. 'It's funny how I've been able to help so many people find happiness but I've not been able to do it for my mother and sister.'

'What about your father? Has he got a new partner?'

Emmie twisted her mouth. 'I've lost count of how many he's had since he broke up with Mum. He seems to be in a new fling just about every month.'

'Maybe he prefers to live his life that way.'

'I guess, but I can't help thinking he's going to end up a lonely old man in the end.'

There was a lengthy silence as they continued moving about the dance floor.

'We all make choices we have to live with,' Matteo said and led her back to the table now the band had stopped their bracket.

And some of us don't get a choice at all, Emmie thought with a deep twinge of sadness.

A few minutes later, Matteo led Emmie into his house and drew her into his arms, his mouth coming down on hers in a surprisingly gentle kiss. Emmie responded by linking her arms around his neck, leaning into his warmth, relishing in the proud rise of his hard male form against her. Her lips moulded to his, moving with the same perfect timing as their dancing had only half an hour ago. Their tongues met and danced a sexy tango that made her blood tingle and race through her veins. His hands went to her hips, pulling her closer to his hardness, a low, deep groan sounding in his throat that vibrated against her lips.

Emmie shivered as his mouth moved from hers to trail a scorching pathway of fire down the side of her neck from below her ear to the framework of her collar bone. His tongue grazed her sensitive skin, sending shooting sparks down her spine.

'I want you.' His blunt statement sent another thrill through her body, an electric thrill that made her inner core coil and tighten with lust.

Emmie licked her tongue along the fullness of his lower lip, a frisson passing through her as her tongue encountered the pinpricks of stubble below his lip. 'Then have me,' she whispered against his lips. 'Because I want you too.'

Matteo pressed an urgent kiss to her lips, his tongue mating with hers in another erotic dance that made her heart race with excitement. After a few breathless moments, he led her upstairs to his master suite, loosening his tie with one hand as he walked her to his bed.

'Here, let me help you with that,' Emmie said, taking his tie in her hand and using it to pull his head down for another kiss.

Matteo groaned against her lips and she opened again to the silken thrust of his tongue, her body quaking with desire. He walked her backwards to the bed, only lifting his mouth long enough to dispense with his tie, tossing it to the floor. His mouth came back down on hers, firmer, with more passionate urgency, one hand going to the back of her dress and releasing the zip all the way to just above her bottom. Her dress slipped away from her like a sloughed skin, and his other hand stroked down the length of her back and then to the curves of her bottom.

Emmie set to work on his clothes but not with quite the same skill and efficiency. She was sure she heard a button on his shirt pop but she was beyond caring. She wanted him naked. *Now.*

Within a few moments, they were both

naked, and Matteo glided his hands upward from her waist to cradle her breasts. She had never considered her breasts the sort that men would want to pay too much attention to, but right then, with Matteo's dark blue eyes gazing at her small form, she had never felt more feminine and desirable. He bent his head to caress her right breast with his lips and tongue, making her almost delirious with lust. His tongue circled her nipple, then he took it in a gentle press between his teeth, releasing it to sweep his tongue around it again. He did the same to her other breast, sending shivers of reaction across her skin.

Matteo guided her to the bed, laying her down. He knelt one of his knees on the bed, his hands resting either side of her hips, a determined look in his eyes. A smouldering look she recognised all too well which sent a river of heat to her core. 'This is all I've been thinking about this evening—tasting you, pleasuring you.' His voice was gravel-rough and so deep she could feel it reverberating in her body as if an invisible wire tied her to him.

Emmie wasn't capable of speech just then. Her anticipation was at fever pitch and, as soon as his mouth came to the heart of her female flesh, she shuddered in reaction. His tongue played her tender tissues like a maestro fine-tuning a delicate instrument, and she came apart in a rush that swept through her like a pounding wave.

Her gasps, cries and whimpers shattered the silence but she couldn't suppress them... nor could she suppress the burgeoning feelings deep inside her. Feelings she had promised herself she wouldn't feel for anyone, must less Matteo Vitale. Feelings that were like tiny fledglings perched high up in a nest, wanting to fly free but sensing the danger of doing so. She had to keep them in the nest. She had to secure the nest, reinforce it, concrete over the gaps so none of those feelings could escape.

They must *not* escape.

Matteo lay beside her on the bed once he had sourced and applied a condom. He ran his hand down the length of her body from her shoulder to her thigh, his gaze focussed intently on hers. 'You are so delightfully responsive.'

Emmie could feel her cheeks warming. Had she been too loud? Too enthusiastic in her response? But how could she help it? He triggered in her such incredible sensations...such forbidden feelings. 'You make it easy for me to respond. I didn't know my body was capable of some of the things you've made me feel.'

He smiled and stroked his hand across her stomach, a lazy finger circling her belly button. 'I could say the same about you…' He bent his head and captured her mouth in a bone-melting kiss, the intimacy intensified by tasting her own essence on his lips. The kiss deepened and then he rolled her over so she was lying on top of him, his hands resting on the curve of her bottom, gently encouraging her to take control. 'This way can increase your pleasure. You can control the pressure and depth.'

The one thing Emmie couldn't control was the growing need for his possession—it was a tight ache inside her flesh, clawing at her with increasing desperation. She lowered herself onto him, shuddering with pleasure as her body wrapped around his steely length. It was erotic, excitingly erotic, and she didn't shy away from it but moved in a perfect rhythm with him. The friction was electric, sending fizzing sensations through her flesh, exquisitely tightening her tissues until there was nowhere to go but off into the stratosphere. The orgasm hit her hard, rocking her to the core of her being, an explosion of sensation that rippled throughout her pelvis. She threw back her head, her hair wild about her shoulders, her cries of pleasure shockingly primal.

Matteo's release followed on the heels of hers and she rode every pounding second of it with another wave of pleasure flowing through her flesh. The bucking and rocking of their joined bodies delighted her all over again. The intimate smells of their lovemaking, their perspiration and body essences overlaid with their colognes and hair products, mingled in the air like a bewitching vapour. Emmie collapsed over his chest, burying her head against his neck and breathing it all in, storing it into her memory.

Matteo stroked his hand down from her neck to the base of her spine and back again. Slow strokes that made her skin tingle and tighten in delight. She had not realised how gentle a man's touch could be. Her first and only foray into sex as a teenager was with a partner who had rushed and, in his hormone-driven enthusiasm, had been a little rougher than she would have liked. There had been small moments of pleasure but nothing like she was experiencing with Matteo. The earth-shattering release he triggered in her was off the scale.

Matteo's touch seemed to read her flesh like someone reading Braille. He sensed all her erogenous zones, seemed to know exactly what pressure and speed she needed to feel maximum pleasure. And she knew it would be a long time, if ever, before she experienced such pleasure with anyone else.

Matteo rolled her over so she was lying on her back, deftly disposing of the condom before taking her in his arms again. His eyes were dark and glinting, his hand coming up to cup one of her breasts. 'I can't get enough of you…' He brought his mouth back down to hers in a skin-tingling kiss, his hand caressing her breast, at the same time sending her senses into overload. He raised his mouth from hers to gaze down at her again, one of his fingers moving in a slow caress along her bottom lip. 'I have to go to Vienna next week for work.' He captured her hand and brought it up to his mouth, his gaze unwavering on hers. 'Come with me.'

Emmie was a little shocked at how much she wanted to go. But was it wise to keep spending time with him? Intimate dinners, dancing cheek to cheek, making love, staying in luxury hotels, as if they were a normal couple. Nothing about their relationship was normal. It never could be. 'Matteo…' She aimed her gaze at his neck. 'I have a business to run and I can't keep flying off to—'

'Look at me.' He tipped up her chin with his finger. 'Tell me what your heart is telling you, not your head.' His eyes held hers in a tight lock, his expression grave.

Emmie moistened her lips, her pulse suddenly unsteady. 'My heart is telling me it would be dangerous to spend too much time with you. And my head is telling me exactly the same thing.'

He frowned heavily. 'Dangerous in what way?'

She eased out of his hold and got off the bed, grabbing at his shirt in order to cover her nakedness. She slipped it on and did up a few of the buttons, her fingers barely able to complete the task. 'I don't want to blur the boundaries with you.'

'We've stated the boundaries,' he said, standing up from the bed and, unlike her, not seeming too bothered with his own nakedness. 'We agreed on a short fling.'

'I know, and I think the shorter, the better.'

He ran one of his hands through his hair from his forehead backwards, his expression a road map of tension. 'Emmie...' There was a grave note in his voice and he came over and took her by the hands. 'The thing is... I think we could make this more than a short fling.' He gently squeezed her hands, his eyes holding hers. 'And I think you do too.'

Emmie pulled out of his hold and began to hunt for her own clothes. 'We might be sexually compatible but that's all.' She found her knickers but couldn't find her bra and pulled back the bed sheets to hunt for it. 'Have you seen my bra? I can't find it.'

'Will you stop for a minute and listen to me?' His frown carved a deep trench between his eyes.

She scooped up her dress and wriggled back into it, twisting her arm behind her back to pull up the zipper. 'I think it's time for me to go home. I'll call a cab.'

'I'm not taking you anywhere until we've talked.' Matteo pulled on his trousers and zipped them up. 'We are more than sexually compatible. I enjoy being with you. I haven't enjoyed someone's company as much as yours before. I've talked to you in a way I have never communicated with anyone else.'

Emmie shoved her feet into her shoes. 'It's my job to make you feel comfortable talking to me. You're reading way too much into it.'

'Are you saying it's all contrived? That you

tell everyone all the things you told me about your cancer and your sister and your parents' divorce?'

'Not everyone, but you're a good listener.' Too good a listener. Emmie had told him nearly everything. Shared so much that it was hard to imagine a time in her life when she wouldn't be able to talk to him any more.

He took her hands once more, his fingers wrapping around hers in a gentle but firm hold. 'Why do I get the feeling you're pulling away from me? Not just physically, but emotionally?'

Emmie painted a false smile on her lips. 'You're the one who doesn't talk about emotions in relationships, remember?'

Matteo brought her a little closer, the warmth of his body reminding her painfully of the cold reality of her situation. 'But I'm talking about them now. I'm asking you to marry me, Emmie. I know you said you didn't want to marry but we could make a go of it. I know we could. We're well suited. You surely can't deny it?'

Emmie wrenched her hands out of his and moved out of his reach, hugging her arms around her middle. 'Please don't do this...' She could barely speak for the anguish rising in her throat. 'We could never be happy.' How could she ever make him happy when she couldn't give him an heir? They might have a great sex life together but how could that ever be enough for a man who needed a wife and heir so badly? She would only hurt him the way she had hurt her family.

'Are you crazy?' Matteo asked in a disbelieving tone. 'Every minute I've spent with you has shown me just how happy we could be. I care about you in a way I have never cared about anyone else.'

'You're not saying you're in love with me?'

His throat moved up and down and a shutter came down in his eyes. 'I'm saying I want to be with you for longer than a fling. I want us to marry and have a family. Not just because of my father's will—although it's part of it, of course—but because you and I make a great team. I know we can make a good life together.'

Emmie raked one of her hands through her hair, her heart threatening to split in two. Pain spread throughout her chest, sending its stinging tentacles to every region of her body. 'Matteo... I can't marry you. It wouldn't be fair to you.'

'Look, I know my proposal is not the romantic declaration of love most women want, but—'

'It's got nothing to do with your proposal,' Emmie said. 'Nor is it because you're not in love with me...or me with you.' Not quite true. She was more than halfway to being in love with him. Her feelings for him had developed robust wings and were desperate to fly free. But she would clip those wings so they couldn't.

'Then what is it?'

Emmie met his gaze. 'I can't marry you because I am unable to have children.'

CHAPTER TWELVE

Matteo looked at her blankly for a long moment, his thoughts twisting and twirling into a tangled knot, strangling his hopes, choking his plans, blocking the pathway he wanted to be on.

He wanted to marry Emmie.

He needed an heir.

Emmie was unable to have children.

He needed an heir.

He cared for Emmie. They were good together. A great team.

He needed an heir.

Emmie was infertile.

He needed an heir.

The whirling of his brain matched the churning in his gut. A strangely painful, burning churning unlike anything he had ever felt before. He wanted Emmie so badly, not just physically, but because the connection he felt with her made him feel whole for the first time in his life.

But he couldn't be with Emmie and keep his family's estate.

He had never felt more blindsided than by her revelation. How could he not have guessed before now? She had told him about her cancer but she had said she was cured. Cured but at a price—the price of her fertility. A huge price for a young woman to have to pay and one he could only imagine caused Emmie great sadness. Was that why she said she never wanted to marry? Was that why she concentrated on finding her clients their happy-ever-after but insisted she wasn't interested in finding her own perfect match?

But there were ways around infertility, many options available that hadn't been there before for couples in their situation. And he wanted them to be a couple, damn it. They already felt like a couple. The camaraderie, the closeness, the connection was not just in his imagination.

He *felt* it.

'But we can have IVF treatments.' Matteo finally found his voice. 'There are so many options these days.'

'But it won't be *my* child,' Emmie said, pressing the heel of her hand against her heart.

'It would have to be someone else's egg. I will never look at a child and see something of myself in its features. None of my DNA will be passed on to him or her.'

'I understand that would be difficult for you but—'

'How can you *possibly* understand?' Her voice rose in despair—a despair that was almost palpable. 'You can father as many children as you like. You haven't had cancer and had all your dreams and hopes taken away. You haven't walked past a pregnant woman or a woman pushing a pram and felt your heart was going to shatter into a million pieces. You haven't held a friend's baby and ached with every fibre of your being because you know you can never hold your own baby in your arms.'

'I might not understand totally but I have lost a child,' Matteo said in a weighted tone. 'And I have grieved every day since for him and for his mother.'

Emmie's arms were wrapped around her body as if she was trying to contain her emotional pain. A pain he recognised because he could feel it grabbing at his guts every time he thought of his late wife and child. His two closest companions were grief and guilt. They followed him wherever he went.

'I know and I'm sad for you. It was a terrible tragedy and one you have to live with for the rest of your life. But, if I married you, I would only add to your pain. You're under enough time pressure as it is. You have to be married and have an heir within a year. Even if I agreed to IVF, it would take far longer than that to become pregnant, let alone deliver a child, and there's no guarantee that will ever happen for me. I don't even know if my body could cope with a pregnancy after all it's been through.'

Emmie's shoulders slumped and she added, 'Even the most in-love couples struggle when going through fertility issues. We don't have the magic ingredient to start with—love. We just have lust, and that is not enough.'

The magic ingredient. Matteo had never been a fan of 'the magic ingredient' of love after the damage he'd seen it do to his father. The magic ingredient caused pain and heartache and vulnerability and he wanted no part of it. But that didn't mean he didn't care about Emmie. He did and he had hoped she would be the solution to his problem. He had started to see her as the *only* solution. But her bombshell revelation gave him pause. He needed an heir. There was no escaping that fact. He had to marry and produce an heir otherwise his family's estate would be lost for ever. It was an impossible situation to be in, a torturous choice—happiness with Emmie and losing his heritage, or keeping his family's estate and losing Emmie.

Matteo picked up the shirt Emmie had discarded and shrugged himself back into it. He needed time to think. He needed a workable solution, one where he didn't have to choose between the two things he wanted so desperately. But how could he think when his emotions were in a state of chaos? His brain was flooded with unfamiliar emotions, ambushed by feelings he didn't know how to handle, let alone identify. 'Why didn't you tell me about your infertility before now?'

Emmie gave him a chilly stare. 'I don't usually discuss my health records with my clients and, at the end of the day, that is what you are—a client.'

Her words were like a cold, hard slap in the face. But any offence taken on his part was hardly justified. She had always been clear about the boundaries. They had drifted into a fling and foolishly, misguidedly, he'd thought it could become something more.

It couldn't.

Matteo searched her features but her expression was stony. The irony was he had used the very same expression many times in the past when a casual lover had asked for more than he was prepared to give. The drawbridge up, the shutters closed, the fortress secure.

'So, it looks like this is the end for us.' He delivered the statement in an impersonal tone. The same impersonal tone he had used many times before when ending a fling. But this wasn't the same as ending any other casual fling. It wasn't supposed to hurt. It wasn't supposed to claw at his chest and shred his guts and make him ache to hold her in his arms and beg her to rethink her answer.

Emmie gave a stiff nod. 'I'll be in touch with a list of potential dates for you.' Her tone was as impersonal as his. 'Thank you for dinner and…everything else.'

Matteo only just managed not to curl his lip. 'Everything else' meaning the best sex he'd ever had. The most intimate lovemaking. Now it was over. Finished. He turned to pick up his car keys and wallet, determined not to show the turmoil of emotion he was going through. A turmoil that made it impossible for him to think of a future with anyone else. 'I'll drive you home.'

'Please don't bother. I can call a cab.'

'It's no bother,' Matteo said, holding the bedroom door open for her.

She moved past him without another word and every muscle in his body wrestled with the temptation to touch her. To hold her. To never let her go.

But he wasn't the sort of man to hold on, to never let go, to beg and plead and fall apart because someone didn't want to be with him.

He was the man who didn't do emotion. He didn't feel romantic love.

And he wasn't going to start now.

Emmie sat silently beside Matteo in the car on the way back to her house. What else was there to say that hadn't already been said? His proposal had come out of necessity, not heartfelt love, and it had been promptly withdrawn as a result of her informing him about her fertility issues. She derided herself for having been tempted into a fling with him. It had only made things a squillion times worse. A fling with a client. How could she have been so stupid? So reckless and foolish to think there wouldn't be a price to pay?

There was *always* a price to pay.

Emmie had taught herself not to want the things most other people wanted and she had been successful in suppressing those desires until she'd met Matteo Vitale. He had upended her life, tempted her into thinking she could have more.

But she couldn't.

That option had been taken from her as a teenager and there was no way of getting it back.

But if he had loved her…

The thought drifted into her mind but she slammed the door on it. There was no way she could marry him knowing she would be stopping him from having what he most wanted. No amount of love could ever change that. In fact, it could even drive a wedge between them in the end. They might have formed a connection, grown closer than she had expected and had amazing sex, but the bottom line was he needed a wife and heir in a hurry and, while she could be that wife, she couldn't provide the heir.

And the biggest heartbreak of all was that Emmie wished with all her heart she could.

Over the next month, Matteo ignored the list of potential partners Emmie sent him via email.

He wasn't in the mood for dating. He began to mentally prepare himself for the loss of his family's estate, knowing it would be impossible to find someone who would suit him more than Emmie. Even if she had said yes to his proposal, he couldn't have Emmie and have the estate too. He loved the estate in Umbria— it was his birthright, the sacred place where his wife and child were buried—but, unless he could fulfil the terms of his father's will, it would be lost. He needed an heir to secure the estate.

But he wanted Emmie.

He could not imagine a time when he wouldn't want her. It was as if his body had decided she was the missing link to his. He couldn't imagine feeling the same intense level of attraction to anyone else.

Matteo threw himself into work but it failed to enthral him the way it usually did. He was in danger of letting down his clients if he didn't pull himself together. He prided himself on his meticulous attention to detail, to finding out the truth behind every account he cast his gaze across. But all he could think about was Emmie's situation, how sad it was for her not to be able to have a child. How cruel life was that so many children were born to inadequate parents and ended up in foster care, while other people like Emmie could not have what they most wanted—their own child. He had seen his own flesh and blood on an ultrasound image, and then only a few months later he had held that tiny, lifeless body in the mortuary. There was no grief like that of losing a child, but close by was surely the grief of not being able to have a child in the first place, especially if it was what you most wanted.

And Emmie did want a child—she wanted one desperately.

Matteo pushed back his office chair, went over to the window of his London office and stared at the crowds of people walking in the streets below. Businessmen and women, people of all shapes and sizes, couples, families— all going about their daily lives while he was up here brooding in a new type of grief state.

Loss and sadness were not unfamiliar feelings…but there was something else that was lurking in the shadowy corners of his mind. From the moment he'd met her, Emmie had encouraged him to talk about his feelings. But talking about them was not the same as actually *feeling* them. He could talk about anger without feeling angry. He could talk about happiness without feeling happy.

But now, he couldn't talk about love without feeling something…something that flickered with a faint pulse in his chest every time he thought of Emmie. As though his frozen heart was slowly thawing, the layers of ice melting away to reveal a confronting truth about himself.

He was not incapable of feeling love.

He had deluded himself into believing he wasn't cut out for commitment. He had fooled himself into thinking he was only interested in casual encounters. He had convinced himself he was more profligate playboy than permanent partner.

But it was all lies.

Self-protecting lies that had shielded him from facing the love for Emmie that had silently, steadily, stealthily grown in his heart. He loved her. Truly loved her. It wasn't just a concept but an actual *feeling*. A state of being. It spread through his chest like something that had finally been set free after a long imprisonment. Free of its restraints, it had planted a seed of hope in the soil of his soul. All he needed now was the sunlight of Emmie. For wasn't she the light in his darkness? Without her, he would wither and fail to thrive. Sure, he could still have an all right life, but it wouldn't be the blossoming, blooming, blissful life he wanted unless she shared it with him.

He could deal with the loss of his family's estate. Lots of people lost their beloved homes, Emmie included. She'd spoken of her childhood home in Devon with great fondness, sold in order for her parents to move the family closer to London. He would learn to speak of his family's estate in the same way and put his regrets to one side. A property was not as important as a person and the only person important to him was Emmie.

But then a doubt raised its head in his brain... Emmie hadn't expressed her feelings for him. She hadn't confessed to loving him. Would he be showing more vulnerability than he had ever shown before by repeating his proposal, by telling her how much he loved her?

But vulnerability was a strength, not a weakness—or so Emmie said. It was a feeling like any other feeling. He could talk about it but it was important for him to *feel* it. To embrace it with courage.

Emmie had a long session with a new client who had a particular request for finding a partner. Harriet McIntosh was a young woman of twenty-nine who had been adopted at the age of two months old. 'I'd really like to meet a man who is also an adoptee,' she said. 'It would be great to have that in common.'

'So…your adoption worked out well?' Emmie asked.

Harriet beamed. 'Brilliantly. I got lucky in the adoption family lottery. My parents couldn't love me more than if they had physically given birth to me.'

'Have you met your biological parents?'

'Only my mother,' Harriet said. 'She was a homeless girl of fifteen when she had me. She left me on a community health centre doorstep with a note attached to my blanket, but the authorities were able to find her through DNA matching later on. She wanted the best for me but knew she couldn't provide it herself. It was a huge sacrifice on her part. I am forever grateful that she loved me enough to do that.'

Emmie had spoken to a few adopted people, some of whom still carried deep sadness about being relinquished, but it was so refreshing… so positive and uplifting…to hear of someone like Harriet who couldn't be happier about being adopted. It made Emmie start to wonder if she was *too* adamantly opposed to adoption as an option. But what if she adopted a child and then got sick again? She would be setting up innocent children for hurt and sadness they didn't deserve.

But you might not get cancer again. Many people go on to live full and healthy lives after cancer.

It was as if two sides of her brain were in deep debate. Could she be the sort of adoptive mother Harriet had been blessed with? Could she embrace the role of parenting without sharing DNA? She loved children. It was hard not to love a child and didn't every child deserve a loving home? The doubts inside her head were less strident, the positives more insistent.

You can be a loving adoptive mother, like Harriet's mother—the sort of mother who cherishes the children in her care. Who loves them as her own, protecting them, shielding them, treasuring them.

Emmie could do that with Matteo...except he didn't love her. And surely the happiest environment for a child would be one in which both parents loved each other? Families came in all shapes and sizes these days. She had made the mistake of thinking there was only one way to be a mother and, because it had been taken away from her, she had ruled out ever doing it any other way.

But there was another way, a wonderful way,

to be a mother. Harriet was living proof of it, speaking so lovingly of her adoptive parents.

'I'm so glad you had such a wonderful experience,' Emmie said. 'I think I have someone on my books who is perhaps a little less happy about his adopted family, but maybe meeting you will help him reframe how he sees them.'

'Oh, great. I can't wait to meet him.' Harriet waited a beat before adding, 'Do you believe in love at first sight? I mean, my parents fell in love with me from the moment they met me. Do you think it's possible in a romantic context too?'

Emmie smiled. 'Yes, I really do.'

After all, she had lived experience of it.

CHAPTER THIRTEEN

HARRIET HAD ONLY just left Emmie's office when Paisley poked her head round the door. 'Your father is here.'

Emmie rapid-blinked. 'My father?' Disappointment trickled through her. It was silly of her to have hoped it might be Matteo instead.

Paisley nodded and added *sotto voce*, 'Maybe he wants you to help him find a partner.'

'He needs no help from me,' Emmie said sourly. 'He's had numerous since Mum.'

'Will I send him in?'

'Yes. But tell him I only have five minutes.'

Emmie stayed behind her desk when her father came in. She couldn't remember the last time they had hugged or shown any affection. It wasn't how their relationship worked these days. Gone were the days of hugs and kisses and playful tickles and words of affection. Her cancer diagnosis had changed her father overnight as well as her.

'Dad, what brings you to my neck of the woods?'

He gave her a sheepish look and placed a hand on the back of the chair on which Matteo had once sat. 'Do you mind if I take a seat?'

'Go ahead.' She leaned her elbows on the desk and steepled her fingers together. 'So, have you visited Natty yet, or has that been a little too uncomfortable for you?'

A dull flush appeared like two flags high on his cheekbones. 'Actually, I was there yesterday and again today.' His throat moved up and down and he continued, 'She seems to be getting a little better.'

'Yes, but it's too early to hope it's permanent.'

'Not much in life is…'

'Parental love is supposed to be,' Emmie tossed back with a speaking look.

Her father seemed to slump in the chair as if an invisible weight he was carrying had suddenly become too heavy. 'You think I don't love you and Natty?' His mouth twisted. 'I think the problem has been I loved you too much. That's why the prospect of losing you hit me so hard.'

'Your timing is way off.'

His mouth twisted again. 'Yeah, I know this is eight years too late, but I still need to get this off my chest.'

'So you can feel better about yourself?'

'So we can be a family again.'

Emmie pushed back her chair and stood with her arms crossed across her middle, glaring at him. 'Are you for real? How can we be a family again when you and Mum can't be in the same room as each other without it turning into World War Three?'

'Your mum and I have been talking over the last couple of weeks and—'

'What?' Emmie stared at him in shock. 'Over the phone? In person?'

'Both.'

'And?'

He took a deep breath and released it in a stuttering stream. 'I told her some stuff I should have told her when we first met. Important stuff about my childhood.'

'You said you had a happy childhood.'

'It was mostly happy.' He swallowed again and scrubbed at his face with his hand. 'My parents, your grandparents, were busy running a business together but they did their best to be there for me when they could. I was close to my grandmother because she took care of me most of the time. She was everything a grandmother should be. That's why I gave you her writing desk. She was a very special person to me. But one day she became ill and was rushed to hospital, and I went with her in the ambulance.'

He blinked back tears and continued, 'I was with her when she died. I was nine years old. I've hated hospitals ever since. I missed her so much. Life was never the same without her. I had to go to boarding school after that, but that's another story.'

Emmie stared at her father as if seeing him for the first time. Seeing the frightened little boy behind the distant and overly critical father he had become. The loving little boy who had lost the person he loved most in the world. 'Oh, Dad, I wish I'd known…'

'It was terrifying when you got diagnosed with cancer. I could see it all playing out again in my mind. I'd be sitting there one day holding your hand, just like I held Gran's, and then you'd be gone…' He lowered his head into his hands and gave a muffled sob. 'And then there's Natty…'

Emmie came over to him and knelt beside his chair, taking one of his hands in hers. 'But

I'm still here and Natty is getting the best help possible. We have to keep hoping she'll make it.'

He raised his bloodshot gaze to hers. 'Can you forgive me for not being there when you needed me? For not keeping us all together? I'm doing all I can to make it up to your mother. She's been marvellous about it. But then, she always was the most amazing person, which was why I married her in the first place.'

'Of course I can forgive you, but why hasn't Mum said anything to me?' It was hard not to feel a little miffed her mother hadn't given her the heads up.

'We're taking it a day at a time, that's why.'

'You mean...you're *seeing* each other?'

Her father gave a wobbly smile. 'I can highly recommend falling in love with the same person twice. I've made some terrible mistakes in my time but the best thing I ever did was fall in love with your mum. And this time, I am not ashamed to tell her every day how much she means to me.'

'But what brought you to this point? I mean, something or someone must have helped you see...'

'I took a good hard look at myself about a month ago. I didn't like what I saw. I'm not sure what triggered it—maybe Natty's relapse. I knew I had to face my demons before they destroyed me.'

'Dad…' Emmie reached for him in a hug at the same time he reached for her. 'I'm glad you're back. I missed you.'

'I missed you too, sweetie.'

It took Emmie a good half-hour to repair her make-up after her father left. She no sooner put on more mascara when she would start crying again. Bittersweet tears for the lost years and the lost opportunities. But she was hopeful her father was on the right track now, learning to embrace vulnerability and show the love he felt but had denied for so long. Emmie glanced at her reflection in the mirror and dabbed at a speck of smeared mascara below her left eye. Maybe she had to do the same thing—stop denying her feelings and embrace them instead.

Paisley tapped on the door and poked her head round again. 'You have another visitor.'

'Let me guess. My mum?' She might as well give up on her make-up repairs.

Paisley's eyes sparkled like twirling tinsel. 'It's *him*.'

Emmie's heart almost leapt out of her chest and landed on her desk. She pushed herself out of her chair on unsteady legs. 'Okay…' She didn't dare harbour any fledging hopes that this visit was anything but a client visit. Not that Matteo had contacted any of the women she had selected as potential partners. She had tried not to read too much into his reluctance to engage with any of the women. She had tried not to think that he might well have found his own potential partner since they had ended their fling. It had happened to other clients of hers. A chance meeting had turned into something else. Had Matteo's problem been solved? Had he found someone who could give him the thing he most wanted?

Matteo came striding in and Emmie had to stop herself running to him and throwing herself in his arms. Her body reacted to his presence the way it always did—flickers of awareness racing across her skin, her heartbeat accelerating, her pulse racing. She hadn't seen him in a month and it looked as if time hadn't been all that kind to him. He looked as though he had lost weight and his eyes had dark circles beneath them, as if he hadn't been sleeping well. Not that she could talk. It wasn't only smeared mascara that had left panda circles around her eyes.

'Emmie.'

His voice was a caress that sent a frisson through her body. *Em-meee*. Oh, how she had missed the sound of his voice! How she had missed seeing him in the flesh.

'Hello.' Emmie adopted her best business-like tone. 'You haven't contacted any of the women I selected for you.'

He came over to her and took her hands in his. 'That's because I only want one woman and that is you.'

Emmie stared up at him, not daring to take another breath in case she was getting ahead of herself. 'But I can't give you a child. And you don't love me.'

His hands gently squeezed hers, his eyes soft with tenderness. 'I do love you. I'm ashamed to admit it took me this long to realise it. You have taught me so much about myself, about identifying my feelings, helping me talk about them. But the one step I missed was allowing myself to actually feel them. But I know what I feel for you is the real deal.'

He drew her closer to his body. 'I know we can be happy together. We can't have the perfect family you dreamed of but we can be together. And that's all I want.'

Emmie flung her arms around his waist, squeezing him so tightly he gasped. 'Oh, Matteo, I can't believe you're prepared to sacrifice so much for me. I love you too. I think I fell in love with you the first time I set eyes on you.' She looked up at him again with a growing frown. 'But your family's estate? Won't you lose it without an heir?'

Matteo stroked her cheek with a gentle finger. 'I would rather lose the estate than lose you. You are enough for me, more than enough.'

Emmie was trying not to cry but failing miserably. 'Oh, my darling, maybe we can have a family. We can adopt or foster. There are so many children out there who need loving homes. We could provide a wonderful home for our children. And they would be ours, wouldn't they? Because we would commit to them the same way we commit to each other—for ever.'

'You'd be open to that?' Hope shone in his gaze. 'Really?'

Emmie smiled and hugged him again. 'I made the mistake of thinking, if I couldn't be a biological mother, then I couldn't be a mother. But I realise now being a mother is primarily about love, not just sharing some DNA. And I can't think of a person I would rather be a parent with than you.'

'You'll be a wonderful mother.' Matteo kissed her lingeringly, leaving her breathless and boneless in his arms. He lifted his mouth from hers to gaze down at her. 'I can't wait to marry you. Don't make me wait. This last month has been torture, not seeing you, not touching you. Every day felt like a lifetime.'

'I won't make you wait,' Emmie said, linking her arms around his neck. 'I feel like such a hypocrite telling you to be open about your feelings when I'd locked my own away. I told you to be vulnerable but I didn't want to be vulnerable myself.'

Matteo cradled her face in his hands. 'I took a gamble that you loved me but were hiding it. I can't say it was easy allowing myself to feel so vulnerable, but I figured losing you would be so much worse.'

'Loving someone is all about facing the prospect of losing them one day,' Emmie said. 'That's why it's so frightening to open your heart. I just had my father here half an hour ago. He explained why he became so distant when I got sick. He was so terrified of losing me that he pulled away. It was a self-preservation move, an unconscious coping mechanism to prevent further pain. He's seeing my mum again. Can you believe that? After eight years of bickering and all-out war, they're actually seeing each other.'

'I'm glad you understand him better. And it just goes to show you should never lose hope.'

Emmie gazed up at him dreamily. 'I didn't realise I could be this happy. I thought I would be alone for the rest of my life. I had even convinced myself I would be happy that way. I had starved myself of intimacy, just like my sister has starved herself of food. It disordered my thinking for so long but meeting you changed everything. You made me realise how much I wanted to love and be loved, no matter what.'

Matteo stroked her cheek again. 'I was the same. Telling myself I was satisfied by casual hook-ups and only finding fulfilment in my work. But we will fulfil each other now. We'll be an awesome team. And we'll need to be, because we'll have a lot on our plate travelling back and forth to Devon and London and Umbria.'

Emmie frowned in puzzlement. 'But why will we be travelling to Devon?'

Matteo's eyes twinkled and he slipped a hand into his jacket pocket and handed her a folded piece of paper. 'For you, *cara mia*, with all my love.'

Emmie took the paper and unfolded it, her

eyes rounding to the size of dinner plates, her heart swelling in her chest. 'Oh, Matteo… You bought my childhood home?' Tears sprouted in her eyes. 'I can't believe it, it's like a dream come true. It's just so generous of you.'

He smiled and wrapped his arms around her. 'You are my dream come true. I love you. And I will shower you with gifts for the rest of our days.'

'I love you so much, it's impossible to put into words.'

Matteo lowered his mouth to hers. 'Then let's put it into action instead, *si*…?'

EPILOGUE

One year later...

EMMIE SAT SURROUNDED by her little instant family and wondered how she could ever have thought she would be any less of a mother for not having physically given birth to her children. Pepe and Paolo, the two-and-a-half-year-old twins, were playing with their father. For Matteo *was* every bit a father to them, as she was their mother, even though they didn't share a single speck of DNA.

Emmie looked down at the sleeping infant in her arms, Isabella, and silently promised Isabella's and the twins' late mother and father she would love and protect these precious children with all her heart for the rest of her days.

The children's biological parents had been tragically killed in a car crash and, with no immediate family Matteo, as the twins' god-father, had stepped forward and been awarded full guardianship. The children had adjusted well to the new living arrangements, being so young, and Emmie was so grateful that, out of such an unspeakable tragedy, she and Matteo were able to provide a loving home for the children.

Matteo came over to Emmie and laid a gentle hand on her shoulder. His gaze was loving and tender, and her heart swelled with love. 'You have the magic touch with Isabella.'

Emmie laid her hand on top of his and gave him a wistful smile. 'It seems wrong to be so happy when the children will never know their real parents.'

'I know.' He pressed a kiss to her forehead. 'Life is a journey between happy and sad moments, but we will make sure our little family has more happy than sad ones.' He stroked a gentle finger over the sleeping baby's petal-soft cheek, then glanced back at Emmie. 'There is no greater gift than promising to love and cherish someone else's children as your own. And these little *bambinos* are very lucky indeed to have you as their mama. And I am the happiest man in the world to be your husband.'

Emmie smiled. 'That's what my father keeps saying to Mum now they have remarried. I still can't believe it, you know. How two people who were at war for so long finally put their differences aside and reclaimed what they'd lost. And Natalie too…' She gripped his hand in gratitude. 'We all have you to thank for her recovery. That private clinic you paid for made all the difference. I have never seen her so healthy or so happy.'

Matteo leaned down to brush her lips with his. 'I would do anything for you, *tesoro mia*. You are my heart, my home, my future, my perfect match. My for ever love.'

For ever love sounded just perfect.

And it was.

* * * * * *

Caught up in the drama of
The Billion-Dollar Bride Hunt?
Get lost in these other
Melanie Milburne stories!

The Return of Her Billionaire Husband
His Innocent's Passionate Awakening
One Night on the Virgin's Terms
Breaking the Playboy's Rules
One Hot New York Night

Available now